SCALES

Jessie Roberts

CONTENTS

1. Chapter One: Beneath the Surface   1

2. Chapter Two: Oddities   8

3. Chapter Three: Safety Issue   16

4. Chapter Four: Erased Self   24

5. Chapter Five: Claimed by the Ocean   31

6. Chapter Six: Left Alone   38

7. Chapter Seven: Feeling Stalked   45

8. Chapter Eight: Hallucinations   52

9. Chapter Nine: Strange Appetite   58

10. Chapter Ten: Poison   65

11. Chapter Eleven: Fanatics   72

12. Chapter Twelve: Storms and Allies   80

13. Chapter Thirteen: Painful Wakening   88

14. Chapter Fourteen: Stupid Actions   95

15.	Chapter Fifteen: Hard Noodles	103
16.	Chapter Sixteen: Had Enough	110
17.	Chapter Seventeen: Defiance	117
18.	Chapter Eighteen: Caught	124
19.	Chapter Nineteen: Consequences	131
20.	Chapter Twenty: Coming Storm	141
21.	Chapter Twenty-One: Hopelessness	148
22.	Chapter Twenty-Two: Accusations	155
23.	Chapter Twenty-Three: Urges and Appetites	162
24.	Chapter Twenty-Four: Unexpected Visitor	170
25.	Chapter Twenty-Five: Fear for Another	177
26.	Chapter Twenty-Six: Tails	184
27.	Chapter Twenty-Seven: Uncomfortable Truths	191
28.	Chapter Twenty-Eight: A Way Out	199
29.	Chapter Twenty-Nine: Unreasonable Witch	206
30.	Chapter Thirty: Plans and Executions	213
31.	Epilogue	222
32.	Follow the Author	224

Chapter One
Beneath the Surface

Ever feel like you don't belong? I do. All. The. Damn. Time. Day in, day out. It's all the same. Then again, it's hard to get noticed amongst a family with seven girls. With three mothers, no less. I know I complain about this all the time, but I really want out of this place. Only one place in this tourist trap keeps me happy, and I don't get enough time there. I'd live there if I could.

"Watch where you're going," Arabella says to Brooke outside my door. It's open, so the words reach me loud and clear.

Arabella has the air of a queen about her. She lets her silence speak, quiet and with a confidence I wish I had. In comparison, I'm clumsy and awkward. Father dotes on her a lot because her grades were always perfect. Right now, her long brown hair is twined in a towel while her eyes of the same color glare at the next oldest sister.

Brooke purses her lips covered in black lipstick. When I try to remember her natural hair color, I can't. It's been way too long since I've seen her short hair anything but vibrant. Blue is the flavor of the week. Her originality is something I am envious of. She makes her mark wherever she goes and turns heads.

"I wouldn't need to be hurrying if Clara wouldn't have spent the entire morning in our bathroom," Brooke says.

"Well, I need to open in an hour. Try to be a little more considerate."

Brooke turns to me. "Why does Naomi get her own room?" When her lips curl into a cruel sneer, I brace myself for what is to come. "Oh, that's right. Her mother couldn't give our father any other children."

She reaches into the room to slam the door shut. I wince and take a deep breath. Arguing never does any good because her replies grow meaner with each one. Despite being the largest house in town, there aren't enough rooms for everyone. Father keeps us together based on who our mothers are. Mine passed away before she could give him more daughters, since that seems like all he can have.

Some townspeople call it a curse that he never got a son, thinking that means the mayor of the town has some deep, dark secret. The three wives disappearing or meeting their end doesn't help. Sighing, I push those thoughts out of my head. When Clara bursts into my room a few minutes later, I almost fall out of my desk chair.

"At that boring journal again? God, you're so annoying. I need your brush," she says without a greeting.

As usual, her blue eyes are screwed up with an expression of superiority. Her blonde hair rests on top of her head in the perfect bun. Out of all of us, I'm sure she's the prettiest, except when she screws her perfect pink lips up in impatience like she is now.

"You broke my last one," I answer.

"You'll get over it. I left mine in the bedroom and Brooke locked me out again. Hand it over."

"My head's been itchy. I may have lice."

Clara jerks back in horror and hurries from my room. "Never mind. You're disgusting."

Emma pops her head in with a giggle. I'd love to know what it's like to be so happy all the time. As usual, her brown eyes sparkle with joy. It's almost sickening.

"That was a good idea. She still hasn't returned the hair dryer she took from me without asking. Maybe she'll leave you alone for a bit."

"One can hope. You have something in your hair."

Gasping, she runs to the mirror. "More paint. Dang. Abigail is hogging our bathroom. Can I grab a quick shower in yours?"

"Sure."

"Thank you!"

As our resident artist runs for my shower, I stand and grab a light sweater. In the hall, I jump to avoid an annoyed Arabella as she rushes for the stairs. She owns her own store, and by the looks of it, she's late.

I stop at the bottom of our stairs to look around. Abigail—never Abby—slams into me from behind, throwing me forward and almost onto my face. Her auburn hair is thrown into a quick ponytail, and anger flashes in her brown eyes.

She doesn't stop. "Why are you always in the way?!"

Lucy sits at the dining room table, her dark eyes hidden by the black hair that falls around her face. She's engrossed in studying for medical exams. Quiet and shy, working with patients isn't what I'd expect out of her, but she's smart enough to make it happen. I walk around the other side to keep from needing to squeeze between her chair and the wall. Even the mayor and owner of the largest tourist business in the town can't afford a bigger house here.

I'm thankful to find the kitchen peaceful. With a sigh, I take a moment to enjoy the near silence. Sound still filters from other parts of the house, but it's muffled here. I walk over to the window above the sink to look over the garden I plant every year in the backyard. It's still bare dirt, but I'm sure green will be sprouting soon.

My bright red hair falls into my face, and I push it away before hugging my sweater around me. It's warm here. Near the water will still be cool. We're just now edging into in-season. Some of the spring chill remains.

"I hope that sweater doesn't mean you're going to the beach again," a deep voice says behind me.

Travis Morgan himself stands behind me. The man cursed to only ever have daughters. The mayor of this town about to wake up from off-season. Controlling father of seven.

I know better than to be truthful with that question. "I just like wearing it because it feels comfy."

His brown eyes hold a look that tells me he doesn't believe a word of it. "Stay home."

"Dad, I'm nineteen."

"And you're my daughter. Don't go gallivanting around town. It's almost tourist season, and people are already trickling in. It's too dangerous for you out there alone. I'll take you to the beach soon."

Pressing my lips together, I nod a false agreement. We both know he won't. Mayor Travis is too important and busy to play in the sand. It'll be another forgotten promise in no time. Not that I can blame him. He has a lot of work and seven daughters to keep him occupied. The only fondness he has for me is because I'm his youngest. I'm far from the favorite and most doted upon.

"Good." He turns to leave, and I realize he might need to take his suit out again soon.

I watch him leave with a sigh. Grabbing a blueberry muffin from the counter, I lean against the marbled surface and pick at my meager breakfast. While I listen to his car pull out of the driveway, I contemplate his words. The only reason he insists we all live here is to control us and make sure we don't become an embarrassment. We range from newly nineteen to twenty-eight, but we're still stuck behind a man that has too much power.

A squabble breaks out in the living room.

"Give it to me!"

"It's mine!"

"You don't need it as much as I do, so it's only fair if you let me have it!"

Clara and Brooke. I'd know the fighting tones anywhere. I pull off another piece of muffin with my fingers and pop it into my mouth. As the fight escalates, I hear a loud thump hit the floor.

"You bitch!" Clara screams at the top of her lungs. "Daddy!"

He's not here, so her cry falls on uncaring ears. If Arabella is the queen, Clara is the princess, spoiled to a fault. Daddy's little girl who can do no wrong, even at the ripe old age of twenty-seven. Shoving the last of the muffin into my mouth, I move toward the door. Lucy watches the archway to the living room and looking exasperated. Must be hard to study with the commotion.

Before anyone can question me, I slip out the front door and onto our deck. The breeze hits me, carrying a salty dampness that isn't strong enough for my tastes. I hurry down the wooden steps. As soon as my feet hit the sidewalk, I turn into the scent of the ocean and begin to walk. It's only three blocks until I reach the busier part of town, full of restaurants, gift shops, and hotels.

It's a straight shot to the ocean, but I detour right by a block to avoid where my father will be. He's probably working hard. One glance at the wrong moment will get me caught. It's still really early, so most of the streetlights are still on. The sun should be peaking above the horizon soon, so I pick up the pace.

Within a few minutes, I'm slipping my shoes off and walking out onto the sand. A few people already walk the boardwalk. We leave each other alone. The grains feel cool between toes, not yet absorbing the coming heat. I curl them to feel the sand shift beneath them. The sun is only a few inches above the distant water.

Perfect.

Walking toward the water, I notice it's calm. I bend down to pick up a pink seashell that will look nice with the rest of my collection. As I walk where the sand is wet, looking for treasures lost at sea, I start to hum the melody from my childhood. After picking up a pretty blue stone, I start to add words to the song.

Mom used to sing this to me when I was little. It's not something I hear elsewhere, so it feels like something between the two of us, one of the few vivid memories of the woman who used to cuddle on the couch with me to watch TV while my sisters played around us. The longer I sing, the louder my voice grows.

Soon, I find myself facing the ocean and singing my tune to the saltwater that's receding with the tide. I don't have the voice to sing in front of people, despite what Emma tells me. Clara and Abigail put too many cruel words in my head for me to believe any kind words. Brooke doesn't help either.

Here, alone on the beach, I feel like I can give proper tribute to the mother who is only left to my memories. The sun comes up to a beautiful song taught to me by a beautiful woman. Nothing exists besides me and the memories. I revel in this ritual every morning, no matter how much my father tries to squash the habit.

A splash startles me enough to stop singing. A shimmer beneath the surface of the water draws my attention. Is it another piece of trash? A fish? Some hidden treasure lost by someone at sea? In the end, I determine it's nothing more than the increasing sunlight reflecting off constantly moving water. I decide to turn back.

Halfway back, I come across a large fish. A large chunk is bitten out of it, as if something lost its meal in the middle of it. Nervous, I look around for what may have left those bite marks, seeing nothing out of place.

As soon as I start humming away my anxiety, I hear another splash. Twirling toward the water, I feel my feet sink into the wet sand. I watch for any sign of movement but see nothing but the familiar shimmer. It seems to be following me. Maybe it's a larger fish that was eating this one.

A prickly feeling washes over me, and my nerves pick up on edge. Glancing around, I see a shadow under the distant dock. The wind picks up, swirling a garment around the shape that reminds me of a flowing dress. I pull my sweat closer with a chill.

Neither of us moves. She may be far away, but I swear she's watching me. Why? I'm just a girl enjoying the beach before it becomes overcrowded. The noise in the sea pulls my attention back. This time, I swear I see glittering scales. Swallowing, I push down the illogical dread that peppers my skin with goosebumps.

Never before have I been frightened of the ocean. Something tells me I should be now. I turn and quickly make my way toward my shoes. Once my feet are protected, I spin to look back over the water. The sun is higher now, hiding any possible glitter of things under the surface. Looking at the dock shows me the strange woman is gone.

For some reason, I don't feel any relief. Instead, dread coils in my stomach until I feel nauseous. I run back home.

Chapter Two
Oddities

"I had the bathroom first!"

"You were doing your makeup. I needed to brush my teeth. You take hours to put your makeup on. Save some bathroom time for the rest of us."

I don't care enough about the argument I walked in on to pay attention to who the participants are. There's always one fight going on at all times. Maybe that's why our father does his best to avoid being home as much as possible. It can't be easy living alone with seven women. The estrogen in this house is at the highest level possible. Hell, even I don't want to be here most of the time.

I shut the front door and pass Emma and Lucille sitting in the living room. The former has her sketch pad out while the latter is watching some medical documentary. As much as I want to keep the argument out of my mind, I pass Abigail and Clara as they continue to argue on the stairs. Squeezing through isn't easy, but I manage. Of course, that means I'm also the proud recipient of two glares.

"You shouldn't even be using my bathroom," Clara says when she's done letting me know how annoying I am.

"Our bulbs need to be replaced."

"Then fix them!"

The door creates a barrier that manages to muffle the yelling enough that I can move it to the back of my mind. Even after all these years, I don't feel like I belong here. I have nothing in common with my sisters, and half of them act like I have the plague. I'd love to be able to spread my wings and fly away from here. Too bad I'm grounded and unable to soar.

Kneeling on the floor, I reach beneath my bed and feel around. The more my fingers come in contact with nothing but dust, the more I scowl. Clara better not have come in and taken it again. She finds my hobby to be boring and unfitting of a daughter of the mayor. As if she has any hobbies that don't include spending the day shopping.

After another minute of searching, I lift the skirt and look under the bed. It's there; just too far toward the back. I drop to my belly to crawl part way under and grab the driftwood box I stash among the dust bunnies. Once it's in my lap, I run my fingers over the rough wood. The last time Clara took it, she ended up with a nasty splinter that became infected. Serves her right.

My mother made this for me, put it together from the treasures she found on the beach. The wood is worn but still beautiful, with my name burned into the lid. Shells, broken glass, rocks, and other pretties are glued to the edge of the lid. Over time, some have fallen off, but I refuse to let the box fall into disrepair. I always glue whatever loosens enough to fall off back in the exact same spot.

This treasure will outlast me if I have a say in it.

In the bathroom, I sit it on the toilet lid and pull out the couple of things I gathered at the beach. The blue stone and pink shell become clean beneath the sink water first. Once they sparkle, I place them in their proper places inside the box. Each type of treasure has its own jar.

I lift the next item, which I think is a shark tooth, and clean it off. My eyes narrow. This isn't from any shark I've ever seen. It's long and needle thin, without the characteristic shark tooth shape. I spin it between two fingers, marveling at the strangeness of it before taking a picture for a later internet search. Curiosity is too strong for me to pretend it's something it's not. It still goes in my jar for shark's teeth since I have no idea what else to do with it.

The last item has too much sand on it. I picked it up on a whim and now run it under the faucet. The muck is stubborn, but I soon see a green glimmer. Maybe it's a shell. I've never seen one that looks like this. There are so many unknowns in the sea that I don't expect to know everything that may wash up.

When I finally get it cleaned off, I furrow my brow. It's a very large green scale, over half the size of my palm. I wonder what this came from. Flicking it with a nail tells me it's tough, almost like glass or thick plastic. This is curious. Could the scale and tooth have come from the same animal?

I look in the box and can't decide where it fits in my collection. Taking a deep breath, I put it in my pocket. For a moment, I think of adding it to my shell collection, but that's not a fitting place to put this mystery. With a huff, I also dig the tooth out and slide it in with the scale. I need a new container.

The box returns to its spot under my bed, and I'm happy to see the stairs empty. In the kitchen, I look through the recycle bin, finding no suitable jars. Huffing, I decide I need something better than a jelly or pickle jar for these treasures anyway, grab my purse, and leave the house once again.

This time, the sun is bright in the sky, warming my skin. I lift my face to the sky, close my eyes, and soak in the joy of outside and fresh air. I can still catch a hint of brine on the breeze, which is one of my favorite scents.

"You're such a weirdo," Brooke says, hitting my shoulder on her way out. "What are you doing?"

"Enjoying the feel of the sun on my skin."

A car pulls up, and she walks over to it. "Whatever. Did anyone ever tell you that you're a freak?"

"No."

"Well, now you know. I figure it's something important to know about yourself."

The back passenger door opens, releasing a cloud of smoke that covers the brine with an acrid scent. I scrunch my face. "Does father know what that smell is?"

"He doesn't, and you better not tell him either," Brooke says. "Quit being lame."

Laughter echoes from inside the smokey space surrounded by metal. Brooke climbs in, and the car speeds away while she's still closing the door. I shake my head. As if Dad would even listen if I told him. He barely listens to anything. After all the fighting I try to block out, I can't say I blame him. Still, an absent father leaves much to be desired.

I stop in front of a few craft stores but shake my head. I don't want some plain jar. As I avoid the town hall, I turn before I can reach the beach. After the oddity of this morning, I'm not looking for more time by the ocean. I still have chills occasionally running along my spine when I think about it.

Could the animal that left the tooth have been the one that abandoned its meal to be washed up on the beach? I pause, contemplating straightening my spine and returning to the sand. There's a crowd already splashing in the waves and bathing in the sun, so it should be safe now. In the end, I shake my head. The odds that the fish is still there aren't great.

Down the street that runs parallel with the boardwalk I go. At an alley, I feel a pull, so I turn down it to find a small shop I have never seen before. *Lenora's Oddities*. Well, this seems to be a good place to go with the day I'm having, so I walk toward the door. A bell chimes as I walk through.

A woman with black hair and dark eyes looks up at me with a smile. "Welcome. What can I help you with?"

I smile back to be polite, a little put off by the cold look in her dark eyes that doesn't match the warmth she's trying to convey. "I've never noticed your shop before."

"It's the only place I could afford in a tourist trap like this. What can I do for you?"

"I'd like to explore."

"Go right ahead."

Those cold eyes follow me as I move around shelves full of beach treasures and jewelry. The chills return, making me shiver in this warm little shack. Bamboo shelves make this place fit in perfectly with the tourist locality that she complained about. I'm not seeing much and consider thanking her before leaving. It might be rude, but I can't take the feel of her eyes cutting jagged trails into my back.

Ready to flee, I spot something that makes me stop. A cute little silver case, decorated with little seashells, catches my eye. It would go so nicely with my box and is the perfect size to fit my mystery prizes and anything else strange I might find in it. A price sticker tells me I can afford it, even if I feel it's a little higher than it should be.

The woman must sense my hesitation. "That's handmade, which is why it's priced as it is."

I lick my lips and consider it. Homemade box for a homemade box. Price may just be worth it. Sighing, I carry it over to the counter and place it in front of her.

"Great choice," she says with the joyless smile. "Planning on putting something in it?"

I look around and feel she might just know. "It looks like you've been collecting things for a while."

"Old hobby."

Looking over all the shiny treasures, I grin. "It's one of mine as well. I found something strange this morning. Maybe you have an idea of what they are?"

"I can take a look."

The scale and tooth come out of my pocket. Her dark eyes light up with the first bit of happiness I've ever seen. Although, even that expression gives me goosebumps. Something feels wrong about this woman, and I'm starting to wonder if I should grab my treasures, thank her, and simply leave without the box.

"You're one lucky girl," she says. "Can I have your name?"

"Why?"

"I want to know who found such a priceless treasure."

Uncomfortable, I say, "Naomi Morgan."

"Morgan? As in Mayor Morgan?"

"Yeah." I hate that my name is a household item. I swear I see a flash of glee in her dark eyes, but it disappears before I can confirm it. My discomfort grows. "And you are?"

"Names on the front of the building, dear."

"Right." Feeling stupid, I swallow hard and almost choke.

In Lenora's hands, the scale shimmers with other colors. It must be something to do with the lighting in here. "What you have here, my dear, is a mermaid scale."

This time, I do choke. At first, I was getting annoyed at someone who only looks a few years older than me calling me dear repeatedly. The word mermaid made that annoyance seem superficial. This woman is crazy.

"Uhh, okay," I say.

She chuckles darkly. "I know how it sounds, but I swear the truth of it. It's a myth passed down for generations in my family."

"What myth?"

Lenora lifts one eyebrow and regards me for a few moments before exhaling. "Well, if it searched for you, then you must be worthy of the tale. Mermaids live deep in the ocean, hidden by magic that no human eyes can penetrate. They fear humans and their violent ways, knowing it's best to stay hidden. Sometimes, though, one grabs their attention. They send one of their scales as a gift."

"Uh huh." Not getting any help here.

She shakes her head. "Didn't expect you to believe me. It's good luck though. Let me put this on a chain for you to wear around your neck at least. You have to admit that it would make pretty jewelry."

That I can agree with. "How much would it cost?"

"One blessed by a mermaid doesn't need to pay for the luck they deserve. Free of charge."

"Okay." It's hard not to draw that word out. Maybe I should just go. Leave the box or pay for it and walk out the door.

I'm not leaving with my scale, and she already takes it to the other side of her counter to drill a hole in it. Fine. I'll finish this interaction and pretend I never found this place after. This woman is crazy.

Lenora mutters over the scale as she makes a hole for the chain made out of seashells. I furrow my brows. When she notices, she reminds me that it's free. I'm not used to people giving me things without expecting me to give them something back, like Clara expecting the use of my shampoo because I asked her to pick up something that I dropped while cooking.

The woman returns with the new necklace and rings up the box. Her store must be old-fashioned because she writes the receipt for my card out and makes me sign it with carbon paper. I grab the tooth from the counter, feeling it pierce my finger.

"Oh, my," Lenora says, grabbing a tissue from below the register.

She pulls my hand over the receipt as she wraps it. A few drops of crimson fall on the slip of paper. When she hands me the top copy, I can tell it already soaked through. It doesn't seem to bother her, so I shrug, grab the small paper bag with the jewelry box, and head out with the scale around my neck. Anything to put this strange day behind me.

Chapter Three
Safety Issue

Abigail yells from the deck, clearly heard through the open windows that let in the precious scent of a distant sea. Too bad the scent isn't strong enough to drown out her annoyance. The smell of searing meat perks up my nose. I inhale, trying to ignore my sisters fighting on the deck while I melt freshly grated cheese into the milk mixture.

Lucy, who is currently cutting vegetables for a salad, hunches in on herself in an effort to appear smaller. She hates conflict, but the way she's tearing the lettuce shows me she's not immune to it. At times, I feel like she's the most innocent out of all of us, which is counter to her high intelligence. Book over street smarts. That's what I'd call it—I think.

Arabella comes back into the kitchen in a huff. Even in the midst of verbal battle, her voice had been too quiet to make out. When Arabella gets angry, her voice becomes low and even to the point an idiot might think she's calm. I shake my head and add more cheese.

"Can you imagine being angry because someone asked you not to overcook the shrimp?" Arabella says, looking for some validation I know she doesn't need to know she's right.

I shrug and continue stirring. Everyone loves my macaroni and cheese, so it's often my job when it's my turn to help cook. I don't mind because it's a reflex now. Lucy mumbles agreement, probably to end what's making her nervous while chopping the tomatoes.

Satisfied, Arabella nods and pulls the freshly baked rolls from the oven. This is dinner at our house. Breakfast and lunch are fend for yourselves, unless one of us decides to do more. Dinner is a communal affair, one that we switch tasks every other day. Half of us cook, then the other half cleans up. This is the only meal our father tends to join us during, even on the weekends.

My skin tingles, so I rub my chest before dumping the macaroni into the cheese. I usually finish this off with a bit of time in the oven to help all the flavors mingle, but Arabella insisted on homemade rolls, and we only have one oven. I still pour it into the casserole dish and place it in the oven for a few minutes to melt a layer of cheese on top.

As soon as I have a minute, I reach up and rub the tingling spot right below my collarbone. It's like an itch that can't be scratched. Clara bounces in to get a soda from the fridge and grimaces.

She takes a long swallow. "Maybe you shouldn't have been on food duty today. You told me this morning that you had lice, and now you're itching your chest. Your hygiene is deplorable."

I sigh. "It's probably just a bug bite."

"Sand flies again? Wait until Daddy finds out that you are still going to the beach every day."

The bright smile she shows tells me that she plans to do just that. Before I can argue, she's out of the kitchen with a giggle. I groan and rub my eyes.

Lucy scrapes the cucumbers into the large salad bowl. "Don't listen to them. I think it's wonderful you have a place all to yourself."

Arabella scoffs. "Please. If she'd learn that following father's rules keeps her safe and comfortable, things like this wouldn't happen. He tells her to stay away for a reason."

Casting her brown eyes downward, Lucy lets her black hair fall to hide her face. She lifts the bowl and takes it out to the dining room as Abigail enters with a large serving plate full of kabobs full of shrimp and steak. Lucy returns to take the basket of warm bread while I take the macaroni and cheese out of the oven.

Arabella throws her nose up, grabs the tray with all the tableware, and leaves the kitchen. Abigail rolls her eyes and follows, with me close behind. As the girls all settle in, Mayor Morgan walks in and takes the seat at the head of the table.

Chatter and petty arguments stop while the food is passed around. I usually keep my meals well-balanced with a slight tip toward the salad, but the kabobs are extra tempting for some reason. I put an extra skewer on my plate before passing them down the line.

"Why do you always cook with these sea bugs?" Clara asks.

Abigail grunts and looks at our sister without lifting her head. "They're not bugs; they're shrimp. Quit being so juvenile. Grow up and eat like an adult."

Clara visibly bristles, her shoulders squaring and her blue eyes narrowing. She tosses blonde hair over her shoulder. "Not everyone is pure carnivore. Maybe you should try being a bit more feminine, but then again, I guess you're the closest thing to a son that Daddy has, *Abby*."

Abigail's head shoots up at the sound of the forbidden nickname. I grit my teeth and ready for the explosion. Clara always pokes the bear, then ends up crying to Daddy about how unfair Abigail is to her. It's sickening.

Dad stands and slaps the table before the obliteration can occur. We all jump. "Enough! I would like one meal without my daughters bickering!"

All of us look at our plates to avoid catching his eye. For an absentee father, he still holds fear and respect from us. An angry voice is all it takes to make us question our life choices. Silence stretches through the room until he says, "Pass the butter."

And, just like that, it's like the argument never happened. I take a bite of my buttered roll before spitting it out. It almost tastes moldy. Glancing down the table, I see that no one else thinks the bread tastes anything but delicious. With a frown, I taste the salad. The vegetables seem rotten. Again, no one else seems to think so. Even the macaroni and cheese doesn't taste right, and I made sure all the ingredients were still good.

Sitting back, I watch everyone else eat without an issue. I grit my teeth and look down at my plate. Maybe I'm getting sick, and it's throwing my taste buds off. That's the only reason I can think of that would explain why my food tastes gross while no one else's does.

My stomach growls, but nothing looks tempting enough to try. Still, I need to eat something before my belly turns into a black hole. I use my fork to pull off a piece of steak, then bring it to my mouth. No one's looking, so I touch my tongue with it before shoving it in. It doesn't taste the same as usual, but it still tastes pretty good.

I chew vigorously, eating all the steak off the kabobs. Poking the shrimp with my fork, I wonder if they'll taste alright too. There's only one way to find out. Flavor explodes on my tongue, and I have to try hard not to moan. I've never tasted shrimp this good. I inhale it all, looking for the serving plate to ask for more.

Excitement falls to disappointment. It's empty. Brooke grabs my plate once everyone has eaten and frowns. "You didn't eat much."

"Guess I wasn't as hungry as I thought."

She rolls her eyes but moves on. My stomach twists with my lie, and I look miserably down at the empty kabob plate before Clara takes it to the kitchen. Emma smiles while placing a piece of strawberry shortcake in front of me. I offer one in return, hoping she can't tell how strained it is.

Ever the happy woman, she nods and moves down to hand out another piece to one of our other sisters. The rest of the table digs in while I stare at my cake. I'm still really hungry, but this doesn't look at all appetizing. I push it away. Maybe I am getting sick. Maybe this is some new virus. I'll have to look the symptoms up when supper is over.

"Hey, Daddy. I found out something that I think you should know," Clara says with sweetness that rivals the whipped cream covering my cake.

I cringe, knowing what's coming next. Dad wipes his mouth and swallows before saying, "What is it, sweetie?"

"Naomi brought sand flies into the house again. I hope we don't need an exterminator."

That clever bitch. I glare at her, but she pretends not to notice. Not only did she just tattle, but she made it seem like concern. This keeps the bad attention off her and puts it all on me.

"Naomi Morgan!" I flinch when the angry dad voice comes back, fully directed on me. "What have I told you about going to the beach?"

I look at the man that sired me but is never around. "It brings me peace, Father."

"I don't care why you do it. I've told you not to!"

"It's just the beach. What's the point of living so close to it if we never enjoy the privilege?"

"You could be attacked or kidnapped. You could be taken away by a sudden riptide and dragged out to sea. Anything could happen. Yet you continue to put yourself in danger by disobeying my orders. Losing any of you would kill me. What were you thinking? What if you were taken?"

I sigh and look down at my hands. "No one is going to take me. I simply wanted to go. Mom used to take me all the time."

"Your mother put foolish notions in your head. You've been collecting things again. Haven't you?"

"They're only little beach treasures. Nothing harmful."

He growls. "If they put you in danger, then they're harmful."

"Seashells won't hurt me."

I look up to catch his face in an ugly grimace. Clara looks quite
pleased with herself. He stops scowling long enough to say, "I told you
I'd take you."

"You always say that, but you're never home. I'm an adult and can
take care of myself. If I waited for you, I'd never be able to hunt for
beach treasures."

His brown eyes turn cold. I swallow, realizing I probably truly
messed up with my arguments. He stands. "If the trinkets you collect
are more important than respecting your father, then you won't have
them anymore."

"What?!"

Without answering, my father stands and stalks out of the room. I
jump to my feet, dodging my sisters as they stand to see some fresh
entertainment. I follow Dad, but he's already up the stairs before I
leave the dining room. I run as fast as I can to catch up. By the time
I do, he's already tearing my room apart.

"Stop!" I scream.

"Where are they?"

"I refuse to tell you."

"She usually keeps them under her bed, Daddy," Clara says behind
me.

When I turn to confront my sister, she ducks behind Emma. My
attention is pulled back to the scene in front of us by the sound of my
father flipping my bed. He picks up the box, stopping in his rage-fulled
anger to run his fingers over mother's work. For a short moment, I

hope this means he still loves her memory enough not to do what I know he plans to.

Too much hope to come true. He pushes through us, keeping the box just out of range of my grasping fingers.

"Please, don't," I say with a small sob.

The group is too big for me to get ahead of. By the time I push my way through, Dad is backing over my box with his car. I scream and lunge, but Emma holds me back. Her eyes hold sympathy while her mouth wields words of comfort and mumblings about my safety. After running it over three times, he sweeps it into a pile, throws it in a bag, then looks over at me.

"I hate you," I whisper loud enough to be heard over the deafening silence.

He flinches before his eyes harden again. "This is for your own good."

Dad climbs into his car with the bag and drives away. I knock everyone out of my way and run to my room. Once inside, I scream in rage, unable to even throw myself on my bed to sob into my pillow. I collapse and sob, crying into my arms.

When I finally calm, I start sweating. I'm suddenly so thirsty that I feel like I've been in the desert for a week without water. My chest tightens, constricting to the point that it can't expand. I can't breathe. Attempting to take a breath does nothing but incite panic. Frantic, I rush to my bathroom, ignoring the strange burn on my chest as the thirst turns into suffocation.

Turning the water on in my sink, I cup my hands and bring some to my mouth. I cough, unable to swallow. The feel of water makes breathing easier, so I turn on my tub and climb in to stick my head directly under the running faucet. Anything to be able to increase the small feeling of relief I just felt. After a few moments under the running water, I'm finally able to breathe again, my lungs fully expanding for the first time.

Panic ebbs as I take a few deep gulps, followed by desperate breaths. Tingling washes over me as oxygen returns to my blood. I gasp and shudder, climbing out of the tub to stand on wobbly knees. My entire body feels heavy and weak. I collapse on my bathroom floor, and the world goes dark.

CHAPTER FOUR
ERASED SELF

A hand on my shoulder startles me out of nightmares full of drowning. I sputter and gasp as if I really just broke the surface of the waves.

"Naomi," Emma says while squeezing my shoulders.

I cough and blink rapidly until I'm able to keep my eyes open. I look up at one of the few sisters I have that has an ounce of kindness in her. My eyes are rough and swollen. "What time is it?"

"A little before dawn. I was worried when you didn't come down for your usual walk."

Trying to laugh hurts. "Didn't you hear our illustrious father last night? I'm *forbidden* from walking the sands again."

"That's never stopped you before."

Shocked, I look up at her. Her blonde hair is pulled up into a tight bun. Her brown eyes hold sadness and concern. Emma brushes my hair from my face.

"You want to get me in trouble?" I ask.

Emma scoffs. "I'm not the others. It's just that I know the beach brings you happiness. You're not like our other sisters, and I don't want to see the brightness in you snuffed out. I can go with you."

I bite my tongue in alarm. "No. Both of us don't need to be in trouble."

"So you're not going?"

"Not this morning. I don't think even the ocean sounds will help me right now."

"Maybe later?"

Trying to offer her a weak smile, I say, "Not today, but I'm not giving up the ocean forever."

She lets out a breath in relief. "Good. Why are you on the bathroom floor?"

For the first time since she woke me, I look at my surroundings to find that I am still on the bathroom floor. "I was upset and not feeling well. I must have fallen asleep like this."

"Do you need to go to the doctor?"

I sit up and shake my head. "I'm fine."

"Are you sure? You didn't seem right at supper either."

So, she noticed. Most of the rest of the people at the table never spared me a glance. Emma always notices more than the others though.

"No," I say. "I'm really alright."

Emma helps me stand, then offers to help me fix my bed. With a weak nod, I follow her out. While she positions to help overturn it, I stop and stare at the space that once held my box.

My sister looks at me. "I'm sorry about your box."

"It's one of the few things I had left of my mother."

"I know. Do you remember what it looked like?"

"Like the back of my hand."

She offers me another smile. "Maybe we can remake it. I'm really good at things like that."

I shake my head. "It wouldn't be the same, and Dad would probably just smash it again."

"Let's right your bed then. The offer still stands and always will."

Nodding, I help put my bed back down. "I hate him."

"I know you do. I wish you didn't have to keep seeing him."

I look at her. "Maybe I should get a job and move out."

Emma laughs. "Arabella has one because she's totally loyal to our father. Lucy will be allowed when she graduates because she will never go against him. He won't let you have one, and there's no way you can move out on our allowance unless you really went without."

Knowing she's right, I feel tears threaten again. When Emma tries to comfort me, I push her away and tell her I'm going to shower now. With one last concerned glance my way, she leaves and closes my door.

My body aches, making me wonder further what happened last night. The extreme thirst, followed by the loss of my ability to breathe. Maybe I really was sick, but I feel fine now. It's possible I ate something bad, and it took time to run through my system. But I didn't eat anything that would have caused that reaction.

At the bottom of the stairs, I catch Travis Morgan exiting for the day. He doesn't spare me a glance, so he misses out on the ice-melting glare I level at him. I used to feel nothing toward the man, no love and affection or loathing and hatred, reserving my judgment to see how adulthood would play out. I'm now feeling the latter.

My precious box, the last remnants I have of my mother, smashed to dust and taken to the dump. No father would hurt his daughter like that. Why does he hold me so tightly if he hates who I am? There's no doubt that the woman dreaming of the freedom of the sea is what makes up my very being. Does he think he can take that away from me?

Growling, I turn and walk toward the kitchen as my stomach twists with emptiness. Lucy once again occupies the table with her books and laptop. I haven't seen anyone else, but I'm also up later than usual. It doesn't matter. I'd rather spend the day away from my hateful sisters.

Lucy offers me a shy smile before the look on my face brings her back to her work.

Muffins, fruit, and other various goodies meet me when I enter the kitchen. Remembering just how terrible everything tasted last night causes me to pause. My stomach grumbles for food, but what if eating sets off the same reaction I got last night? I pick up a blueberry muffin and give it a quick sniff. It smells alright.

I purse my lips in thought, wondering if I'm willing to attempt eating when it went so horribly last time. My stomach kicks me into a decision. With a sigh, I pick off a small piece from the top—my favorite part. As soon as it hits my tongue, I pull it out with a wince. It takes me a moment to realize it tasted fine.

I'm now braver, dropping the small piece into my mouth and letting it melt on my tongue. It tastes like sugar and blueberry. Convinced that means I'm better, I devour the muffin and grab another. This time, cinnamon bursts on my tongue. I groan in pleasure. After three more, I look in shock at the wrappers lying on the counter. Did I really eat that much?

Guess steak and shrimp weren't enough to fill my stomach last night. I'm finally full and not in the least bit sick or distressed. I feel well enough for a walk. Just in case, I fill up a tumbler of ice and water before walking toward the door.

Brooke bursts through as I'm getting ready to leave. "Hope you're not going to the beach today. We know what happens when you do."

I scowl and turn for the door. "Don't worry about me. Our father made my consequences quite clear. Worry about yourself."

"Is that a threat?"

"It's a cautionary warning."

Before she can answer, I step out onto the porch and slam the door shut. I hear her call me a freak, loud enough to reach me through the solid wood between us. Rolling my eyes, I trot down the porch and stop in the well-manicured grass. Rain threatens, so I wonder if a walk is the great idea I once thought it was.

Clouds as dark as my grief move swiftly across the sky, as if trying to keep ahead of the destruction they bring. Fitting. I have more in common with storm clouds than I first thought. I need sunshine, but it's nowhere to be found.

That's why I mentioned running off on my own. Too bad Emma is right. Father gives us enough money to pay for our needs but not enough to save up. No place will hire us without his approval, which he won't give. I'm as stuck as any of them. Why does he feel the need to control us as he does? To feel powerful? To keep his property—as he sees us—close?

I huff and drop my gaze from the sky. Something glimmers in the driveway, so I walk over to see what it is. Maybe at least one of my treasures avoided destruction.

The glittering pieces turn out to be small slivers of jagged glass. "I hope he flattens a tire on them."

Bending to bring myself closer, I see a few splinters, all that's left of the box my mother crafted for me with love. Maybe the rumors are right. Maybe he had something to do with her death. She gave him what he wanted, another daughter to possess and bully. She was no longer useful to him.

I press my lips tight, breathing through my nose with deep inhales and exhales. Did he ever love any of his wives? Does he love his daughters at all? Last night's temper tantrum is enough to give me the answer to that last question. If you love someone, you don't destroy a piece of their heart simply because they didn't obey your wishes.

The remains of crushed shells shimmer in places on the dark asphalt. Something white grabs my attention. It's lodged in a crack where it wouldn't be easily swept up. My fingernail digs in, and I pull my finger away from the crack with a hiss. A small pinprick of blood wells right beside my nail. I suck on my finger until it stops.

Ready to give up on whatever was sharp enough to cut me, I stand. If it's that sharp, it probably is only a piece of shell or something else he shattered. Something deep inside doesn't let me walk away. Maybe the thought of leaving even a piece of my treasures behind hurts too much. I know I want them back, so this is possibly my unconscious unwillingness to leave it.

This time, I try the other side in hopes that it's not as sharp. I tear my nail and scrape the tip of my finger, but I manage to get one end out. I wiggle and pull until I'm sure whatever this is will shatter and cut me more. It doesn't. Thanks to the sudden freedom of my treasure, I fall back, land on my butt with an oomph, and barely manage to keep myself from ending up on my back.

Sitting to breathe for a few moments, I hold the object tight between my fingers without looking to see what it is. I'm afraid it's some random piece of trash that was there long before my box was run over. It's too painful to look to find an animal bone or something else.

After my lungs fill one last time, I look at my fingers before exhaling loudly. It's the strange tooth. Out of everything, this unknown animal tooth made it through the deadly weight of my father's tires and wedged itself where it would be safe. I turn it in my fingers with wonder, grabbing the scale under my shirt with the other hand.

My last two beach treasures. I worked so hard to collect all of them, and these are all I have left. A lifetime of love and consistency, lost to the temper of a man who doesn't like being disobeyed. It will take forever to find so much again.

And how am I supposed to do that if I let Father win? I'd have to find another box and hide it somewhere else. Standing, I look back at the house, then at the shimmer of my destroyed work. Emma is right. This is part of who I am, and it can't be destroyed so thoroughly... unless I let it.

Determination fills me, and I turn toward the salty breeze. Travis Morgan won't win. He won't erase my mother. I won't hide the woman I am. Who does he think he is? Just because he's the mayor and my father doesn't give him the right to snuff out my individuality. This isn't just a hobby. This is a habit given to me by the woman I lost so long ago, an integral part of my being.

Gritting my teeth, I walk down the driveway, onto the road, and make my way toward the beacon that has called to me all my life. I will follow it as I have always done. He can't stop me. He can't turn me into someone I don't want to be. He's welcome to try, but I won't give up.

Chapter Five
Claimed by the Ocean

New box under my arm, a simple one I found in a thrift shop, I stop on the boardwalk and look at the crowd that covers the sand. I sigh, realizing I'm not going to find anything at this hour. Sunbathers stretch out next to children building sandcastles. Couples walk along the water's edge, feeling the tide come in.

After a quick storm, the sun now shines again. I can only wish my own darkness could be so fleeting.

Anything that might have been washed up on this sand is probably already gone, even anything new from the recent fierce weather. If I want to rebuild my collection, I'll have to resume my predawn treks. That means avoiding Dad and slipping out without anyone noticing. Possibly leaving earlier would help. All my sisters are too busy fighting over bathrooms to notice me slinking through the house. Well, slinking may not be a good idea.

Although, I'm here, so I might as well see if I might be lucky enough to find something. Tucking the box tighter under my arm, I walk onto the sand. It's a bit harder to walk with sandals on, but the small grains will have already stolen the heat of the sun and begun drying. Besides, leaving them in their usual place might tempt someone to steal them. I don't want to waste my allowance by buying a new pair, and I'm not walking home in my bare feet.

I weave between tourists and locals. Once I reach the lapping water, I stare with sadness at my sandaled feet. I'd prefer to feel the bubbles and cool liquid lapping at my toes. Looking around reminds me that the audience is too large for a song, further making me feel depressed. Instead, I hum the melody under my breath. This will have to do until I resume my morning stroll tomorrow.

The familiar shimmer sparkles in the distant waves, causing me to pause and shield my eyes against the sun. It's too far and too bright to make out, but that doesn't stop me from trying. I feel like if I can just look hard enough, I can make out whatever it is.

Something hits me from behind, nearly throwing me into the water. With a startled scream, I pinwheel my free hand while clutching my box with the other. Strong hands reach over to keep me from falling headfirst into the salt water. A teen laughs and apologizes before bending down to pick up a football lying in the sand.

He's gone, throwing the projectile back toward his buddy a little down the beach. Grumbling, I check my new box to ensure it's not damaged. It's painted wood, not nearly as beautiful or meaningful as the one my mother made me. It's still big enough to fill with beach goodies; if I ever find any.

Glancing back at the pair tossing the ball between each other, I sidle the opposite direction to make sure I won't get run into again. I scan the waves, looking for the glimmer of whatever grabbed my attention before. It's gone. Sighing, I look around for a likely place to find something to make my box a little less empty. The dock might be a good place.

The shaded area is cool from lack of sun and still wet from the rains. My feet slip in the sand while I navigate around the large pillars. One has a tuft of dark hair snagged on a splinter, probably a lover's tryst or something. Crouching, I dig around in the sand a bit, finding a few whole shells and a lot of broken ones. A red stone goes into my box as well. Everything needs to be washed, but I'll do that when I get them home.

Decay reaches my nose, which makes me press the back of my hand against the offending part of my face. With thoughts of that bitten fish in my mind, curiosity makes me follow the scent. I squeak and jump back, gagging at the mess of blood and wet fur. In a hurry to reach the sunlight, I stumble backwards.

It was a dog. Something had bitten chunks out of it and ripped out its insides. Gasping, I take a few deep breaths of clean air, trying to push the sight out of my mind forget the rancid smell. The fact that it has a collar on makes me wonder where it came from and worry a young child is looking for their beloved pet.

Spinning, I move my gaze over the crowd. No one seems to be looking for a lost dog. I could get closer and see if I can read the tag, but the thought of getting that close makes me feel sick. I stuff the guilty feeling down and turn to walk back the way I came. It might be better if the child missing their loved pet doesn't see it in this condition.

That's one excuse to simply walk away that I can live with. I know I wouldn't want to see it. That was terrible. The maggots in the eyes aren't helping. I feel like I need to flush my eyes out to get the images out of my head.

Screams pull my attention from the dead pet. A group of people huddle around the edge of the water, so I rush over to see what's going on. A few others pull a man from the water while another yells that he was dragged out to sea by something. The bottom half of his leg is gone, and he's unconscious.

When I see his face, I gasp. It's the teen that hit me on the beach. Anyone in the water is getting out quickly, but no one else seems to be attacked by anything. The lifeguard runs over, talking too fast to understand on his radio. I back away to let him work.

I watch him create a tourniquet to stem the blood gushing from the kid's stump. He looks so pale that I worry he's already lost too much blood. Sirens echo in the distance as I make my way to the back of the crowd. The smell and sight of blood is making me uncomfortable as the water washes it off the sand.

EMTs rush onto the scene. I look back to see my father's car pull up by the pier. I mutter a few curses too low for anyone to hear and walk down the beach in the opposite direction. If he destroys this box, I can't afford to buy another. Even if I did, he'd probably cut my allowance more to keep me from purchasing more in the future.

The skin beneath the scale against my chest burns, and I pull it away with a grunt. I dodge behind the public restroom and pull the shirt away from my skin. The scale shimmers like it did in Lenora's hands, colors changing as they run over the surface, and the skin beneath it is red. I touch the spot with a hiss of pain.

Pulling the necklace over my head, I place it in the box and wonder how it got hot enough to burn. It was under my shirt, so the sun can't be the culprit. I rub the spot with my palm as I look around the corner of the concrete building. As soon as the mayor closes in on the chaos, I turn and walk as quickly as possible without looking like I'm running away from the scene.

I follow the boardwalk, then cut down one of the side streets. The scuffle of a shoe makes me look forward instead of behind. Lenora stands at the end of her alley and smiles at me. "Why the hurry, Naomi?"

My sandal straps cut into the top of my feet as I skid to a stop. "A teenage boy got his leg eaten in the ocean."

"Did you have something to do with it?"

"No!"

"Are you sure?"

The look in her dark eyes makes my heart skip a beat. She's anticipating something, looking for something in particular. It's almost like

Lenora can see what happened through my eyes. I snap the connection our gazes make by looking away.

"Yes, I'm sure," I say.

"Then why are you running?"

"My father—" I pause, not sure why I was about to air my family drama to a creepy stranger that has a habit of making me uncomfortable. "It's not important."

"If you didn't have anything to do with what happened, you shouldn't run. It makes you look guilty. If you did, you still shouldn't run. It makes you look guilty."

Something in her voice makes me look at her again. "You make it sound like you know."

Lenora smiles in a way that sends shivers down my spine. Her eyes gleam in challenge, as if daring me to ask the question that goes with that statement. I snap my mouth shut, refusing to utter what's at the end of my tongue.

She chuckles. "How is the box working out for you?"

"Uhm, my dad took it from me. I'm pretty sure I won't get it back."

"Why's that?"

"Why did he take it, or why do I not think I'll get it back?"

"Both."

I look away again, discomfort growing to wicked levels. All I want to do is get home and hide away to process all that has happened. "Again, it's not important. Simple family drama."

"I see."

My gaze snaps back again. It sounds like she actually does. I open and close my mouth a few times, unable to find any words that make sense right now. I look toward home and consider saying my goodbyes in a hurry.

Lenora is faster. "Did the injured boy interact with you at all?"

I furrow my brows. "He ran into me while playing football."

"Did you get hurt?"

"No. I was only annoyed."

"That's probably why they were able to pull him out."

"What are you talking about?"

The creepy gleam returns to her eyes. "The ocean claims those it wants as its own. If you have the sea in your soul, it knows. I can smell it on you, so I know you belong to the waves. The ocean looks after its own."

"That's crazy."

"So some say."

I snap my lips together before I can say something even more insulting. I just called her crazy. She seems pleased, but my instincts tell me that angering her is dangerous. "I need to get home."

Lenora lowers her head, then raises it in one single nod. "Farewell, Naomi. I'm sure we will meet again. I have more jewelry boxes if you need them."

"I'm fine. Thank you."

I hurry away, glancing back to see her watching with a malicious grin that dries my mouth. My feet almost break into a run until her previous words hit me. Walk, don't run. I slow and act like I'm not fleeing from a crime scene. I've done nothing wrong.

As soon as I turn a corner, I feel the pressure on my chest release. The goosebumps covering my skin slowly absorb back in. I breathe deep to ensure I can do so because Lenora's grin left me breathless. Something is really wrong with that woman, and I will do my best to prove that she knows nothing of me. I won't see her again if I have any say in it.

Once I reach home, I rush up the stairs, ignoring the bickering going on in the living room. I close my door and lean my back against it. Today didn't happen. It couldn't have.

The dog, then the teen. I won't even think of Lenora. None of it happened. I have to be having a nightmare. I'm still collapsed on the bathroom floor, probably with a raging fever causing strange dreams. This day can't be real.

I rub the spot on my chest again. Nothing but a dream. That's all it is. No other explanation makes sense.

Once I calm down, I take the time to clean my new treasures. I'll find out if it's a dream or not later. If it's not, these need to be cleaned. I refuse to touch the scale as I add the pebbles and seashells back to their freedom in the box. I'll need to raid the recycling again, but everything is fine in the box without being separated for a while. Fishing the strange tooth from my pocket, I add it as well.

A high cupboard above the toilet finds itself as my new hiding place. I cover the box with a few old towels before climbing down to the floor. No one will look there. I'll just have to make sure that none of my nosy sisters bursts in, thinking I'm in the shower or on the toilet. It happens a lot more often than it should because no one understands why I get my own bathroom.

Taking a few deep breaths, I decide to look for something to eat for lunch in hopes that the distraction will wash the horrors of the day away.

Chapter Six
Left Alone

I make my way out to the lone picnic table in the middle of the yard. We have more tables stored in the gazebo for parties, but Dad decided that we squabble too much to have more than one cluttering the lawn at all times, which I feel does the exact opposite of what he expects it to. My plate contains a simple ham and cheese sandwich with extra mayo. I wasn't in the mood to chop lettuce or slice a tomato, so the word bland got thrown at me by one of my sisters. I didn't care enough to pay attention to who it was.

All I want is peace, which is hard to find in this place.

The wind picks up, causing me to stuff my napkin under my plate to keep it near. I take a moment to lift my face to the sky and enjoy the feeling of the air moving over my skin. The sun now hides behind more clouds, promising more rain to come. It seems that the quick storm earlier today is only an omen of what's to come. I'll remain outside as long as I can.

Eating my sandwich, I try to put every strange and uncomfortable thing happening behind me. I shove it all into a deep, dark hole inside my mind. It's unfortunate that hole isn't a void that holds everything forever and doesn't let it come back. I'm sure everything stressing me out will return to haunt me. Right now, I simply want calm, so I clear my mind.

The wind picks up faster, bringing the sweet scent of our blooming tree to me. I'm not sure what kind of tree it is, and I never really cared to research it. All I know is that the light pink blossoms throw petals all over the place, including onto the last bite of my sandwich. I clear the soft dew drop shape off my final piece and pop it into my mouth.

When the air brings in a mist this time, I groan and look at the book I had hoped to read outside. My eyes find the giant gazebo. Leaving the plate to be washed by the incoming rain, I pick up my horror novel and make my way to safety from the falling water moving in.

Squeezing between tables is difficult, but I find a spot close toward the center to settle down. Musty staleness takes over the smell of fresh air, brought on by the tight space and incoming clouds. I find a cushion to lean against and settle myself on the floor between two tables, out of sight and out of mind.

Privacy is hard to come by without sequestering myself in my room, so I do what I can. I flip the cover of my new book and decide to lose myself in the darkness within these pages. Maybe the shadows in my life won't seem so bad if I'm reading about someone that has it worse.

Thunder echoes, followed by a flash of light. I consider going back inside but remind myself that this gazebo is big enough to keep me dry. Even the lightning won't destroy the peace I desire. Rain hits the roof hard enough to be heard through the wood. Perfect. A relaxing sound for a relaxing activity.

About two chapters in, the storm eases a bit. Footsteps bring my gaze up, and I climb to my feet. Lucy startles at my appearance. "Sorry. I didn't mean to scare you, Lucy."

"I guess you had the same idea as me. I had to get out of there."

"Who's at it now?"

"Who isn't? Uhm, would you mind if I settled in to get some schoolwork in?"

"Of course. I don't own the gazebo. Having less caustic company may be pleasant."

She smiles, brown eyes shining with delight. While Arabella gains our father's trust enough for a job from being totally loyal, Lucy buys it with her meekness. She'll live here without threats for as long as our father wishes, or until he's dead. Whichever comes first. I'm betting on the second option.

Lucy moves a few chairs until she's able to clear a spot big enough for her schoolwork. The companionship is quiet and comfortable as she settles in. I return to my seat and book. I lift the straw of my cup to my lips to sip a little sweet tea. No better way to spend an afternoon.

I'm unsure how much time passes before I'm halfway through my book and Lucy is packing up. I crane my neck to look at her and say, "Got what you needed to finish done?"

With a shy smile, she nods. "Took longer than I thought, but my presentation is ready for Monday."

"Good."

She pauses, as if unsure she wants to talk to me. "Can I ask you something? I know small talk annoys a lot of people."

"Sure. I won't bite your head off like the others."

Lucy's relief tells me her uncertainty was because she didn't think I'd want to talk to her, not the other way around like I first thought. "Why does Father fear the beach?"

"Absolutely no clue. It's not like I even go into the water. Tourists tend to leave me alone. His fear seems more like a phobia he's pushing onto me."

"I know he mentioned tourists, but I never heard him mention the water. Is that dangerous?"

I shrug. "I never go in far because I can't swim. I mainly visit the beach to hunt for treasures. Dad never let me learn how to swim or surf, so I'm sand bound. I guess sharks are always a worry."

Lucy's brown eyes widen with alarm. "Do they come that close to the shore?"

Visions of a missing leg and blood swirling in the water as it's washed out of the sand flash before my eyes. I wince and look away. "I think it's possible. Lucy, you're pretty smart. Do you believe in mermaids?"

"Oh," she says. When I turn back to her, her hand is covering her mouth. "I never knew you believed in mythical creatures."

"I don't. I'm just curious what you think. Someone tried to convince me they're real earlier."

She laughs. "There is no magic, only science. I guess it could be possible since we haven't explored much of the ocean, but I can't find it in myself to believe in them."

"Me either," I say with a sigh of relief. While Lucy walks away, I consider the feeling. No matter what Lenora believes, mermaids are simply imagination and wishful thinking. I'm not sure why her answer makes me feel better to have that confirmed. The creepy woman must have gotten under my skin.

Who am I kidding? With everything happening recently, that's not hard to do. I'm more than a little unsettled, so my mind is questioning everything. What sits in my new box is nothing more than a pretty piece of jewelry. Maybe someone made it and lost it to the waves. That makes a lot more sense than believing in magical creatures.

Sighing again, I close my book and stand with the next grumble of my stomach. The storm has passed, so moving back to the house is safer for the bound paper in my hands. It should be about time for supper, and I'm on cleaning duty today.

Wet grass tickles my sandaled toes and brings a chill that produces goosebumps. Dampness hangs heavy in the air, making it feel thick. After grabbing my plate from the picnic table, I make my way up the porch and into the house. When no cooking scents greet me, I look around confused.

Arabella comes out of the living room with a few cups that someone must have been careless with. "Why do you look like someone has given you the universe's greatest mystery?"

"I don't smell food."

"Don't tell me you forgot?"

"About?"

She rolls her eyes and stares at me with annoyance. "The banquet tonight? Founders' Day? Father is the guest of honor, and we're to be there."

I flinch. I did forget. Posh events aren't really my thing. If I would have remembered, I would have found an excuse to be gone before someone could remind me. This is the last thing I want to deal with tonight.

Arabella shakes her head. "Clara bought everyone dresses. Yours should be on your bed."

My oldest sister stomps away, muttering under her breath about ungrateful daughters. I send her a glare before making my way toward the stairs. I've been seen, so I have no choice but to attend. Father will have a limo hired and everything. This is going to be a long night, and I'd rather stay home to finish my book.

As mentioned, a dress greets me on my bed when I walk in. It's pretty, but I hate dressing up. Give me shorts and a tank top over a dress any day. Sleeveless, the top is form-fitting and dark blue. The skirt is a lighter blue material that shimmers and flows.

I run my fingers over the fabric and feel a small lump under the midsection. Curious, I dig a box out from under my dress. A scribbled name is etched on top. If it wasn't for the fact I expected it to be mine,

I doubt I'd be able to read the harshly scrawled lines. Of course, it's open. Nosy sisters don't let anything unknown get by them.

Flipping the flaps open leaves me to grimace at what I find inside. The silver with sea treasures fastened to it looks exactly the same as the one I lost to Dad's temper tantrum. I lift the lid to find a folded piece of paper.

Don't let your father take this one. A beautiful necklace deserves a beautiful jewelry box.

~L

I grimace. Seriously? With how expensive that first box was, I wouldn't have expected her to give me another for free. Worse than that, I don't want to owe her anything. Avoiding Lenora is a top priority, so why is she making that so hard to achieve? Maybe I can pretend I never received it. Then I won't need to stop to thank her out of politeness.

Slipping into my dress, I put the box out of my mind for now. I walk over to my hiding place and pull out my necklace. The scale really would go well with this dress, not that I can let my family see it. Screw it. I slip it on and slide it beneath the bodice. The shell necklace is visible, but nothing can be seen at the end of it. That should be good enough.

"Five minutes, ladies! Let's go!"

The call to hurry echoes through my door. My eyes fall on the box when I exit my bathroom. I debate possibilities and decide my earlier idea has the most merit. I stuff the trinket back in the box it was delivered in and carry it down the stairs with me. A limo does wait in front of the house, as expected. I detour to the front of the garage, hesitate for only a second, then toss the box into the garbage can.

I don't want anything from Lenora. She doesn't need to know I tossed it. It's ridiculous that she can't take a hint. I want nothing to do with the creepy woman. Slamming the lid on the can, I hurry over to the limo before Dad can grow impatient. It's time to act like a well-put-together daughter and mind my manners. Not looking forward to this.

Chapter Seven
Feeling Stalked

The limo pulls into the front drive of one of the largest and most expensive hotels in the town. Hanging back, I let my sisters follow Dad out first while I watch. I hate these events. There will be news reporters outside and locals kissing my dad's ass to get some permit approved or something like that. They'll jockey for attention while bachelors try to woo the daughters of the illustrious mayor. No one else knows the iron fist Father uses to keep us single and home. That would be a PR nightmare.

I sometimes wonder what would happen if we'd spill the beans about the treatment we receive. Would he deny and destroy our characters to keep his secret? Would we be disowned and shunned? Where do I find even a small shred of loyalty not to drag his name through the mud in the name of freedom?

Emma slips out, leaving the limo empty besides me. I find myself wishing I could just pretend not to be here and ride away. I almost snort because I know Dad is probably waiting impatiently for me to show my face. All daughters will be accounted for.

Ignoring the flash of the cameras, I crawl as gracefully as I can from the exuberant vehicle. My head instantly turns toward the crashing waves to my right. In the darkness, I can just make out the darker swells of water with the white tips glimmering from the lights along the boardwalk. The salty smell makes me long to stroll the sand, not spend the night in strategic conversation with people I have no wish to talk to.

Emma calls my name, and I follow along, happy to be in the back of our group with her. Bright lights make me blink as we enter the lobby. Mayor Morgan is on full display today; shaking hands, waving, and smiling at those he feels deserve it. Everything is a move to make important people happy and keep his position secure. Politics... my least favorite activity in the world.

Every part of me wants to find a corner to hide in, but I know better. Father will expect us to follow him around like a flock of colorful birds. We'll all act like loving daughters while he preens his feathers in front of benefactors. We'll eat an elegant dinner, then be dismissed one by one. Even then, I'll be expected to mingle and flirt. We can't be anti-social and ruin Dad's chance at reelection.

In this respect, seven smiling women who adore him can only be good for his campaign. My face hurts with the effort to keep my lips turned in a pleasing way by the time we sit. A speech is made, which Dad follows up with one of his own. I pay attention to none of it. All I want to do is go home, but we will be here until the end, then we will be expected to smile while every person stops him on the way out to get one more word in.

Dinner is a fancy affair, some sort of fish smothered in some sort of white sauce. While apprehensive at first, I do find the flavor delicious. Although, I could do without the sauce. I don't touch my fancy salad, too nervous to be done with the food. I'm surprised the fish even kept my attention long enough to devour it in a lady-like manner.

Again, I almost snort—an unbecoming sound of a sophisticated young lady. I would never call any of my sisters lady-like. Not even close. Not even the ones that try to be. We're all a mess that likes fighting with the other disasters. Father needs to see at some point that we need our freedom. Life will be so much more peaceful then.

This time, as we stand again and mingle, I watch the other six peacocks flutter away, one by one, to leave me alone with our father. I try not to dig my teeth into my lips and try to inconspicuously look for an excuse to flee. Waiting for his permission to move along keeps my body tense and my ears straining.

For a short minute, the flow of people stops. He turns to me. "Naomi, we need to talk."

I flinch, looking at the hands I clasp in front of my stomach. "This doesn't seem like the place to do so."

"When I'm home, you're not. If you are, you're hidden in your room. This is the only place I feel we can discuss what needs to be discussed."

My teeth clack together as I bite back what I have to say because another citizen walks up to us. Dad smiles and greets him as if not about to lecture his most defiant daughter. I take a few deep breaths to calm myself before the interloper slips away.

"I'm not being hard on you to be mean," he says once the coast is clear again. "I want you to be safe."

Pain radiates with my clenching jaw, so I force it to relax. "I can take care of myself, Dad. I promise never to let someone kidnap me, and I promise not to fall and break a nail."

Father flinches slightly at my angry tone; only a bit to keep from destroying his appearance of talking sweetly to his youngest. Remembering where we are, I bring back the forced smile. It's hard when I want to stomp away from this respected man without any further words together. Why can't he just leave me alone?

"I know you hate me right now," he says after a pause to greet a passerby. "What I'm doing is for your own good."

Tonight seems to be a night of holding back snorts. "You're doing what you feel will keep your image what it needs to be for your goals. I simply don't understand why that includes keeping me from the one place I feel most at peace, then destroying my last memories of my mother."

At the start, Mayor Morgan's face twitched with the force needed to keep his happy visage. Toward the end of what I said, he looks down at his feet to compose himself before looking back at me. "I do not wish to make you unhappy. I know the house and your sisters can be a bit much, but you need to trust me."

"Would you trust someone who seems to want to keep you prisoner and destroys the one thing that gives you joy?"

Dad gives a silent huff and looks away to wave at someone calling his name. This is ridiculous. We can't keep up a worthy argument like this, which only proves the fact that this isn't the time for a heated discussion. Maybe that's the real reason he's choosing now. I can't get mad and stomp off in anger. He's keeping the conversation calm to avoid my temper.

Well, screw that. If he thinks he can use the public to muzzle me, he has another thing coming. I open my mouth to say something particularly nasty when a voice makes me snap it shut.

"Naomi and Travis Morgan."

Every single muscle in my body tenses while my joints lock in place. If I thought this situation was unfavorable already, that voice makes it worse. It's bad enough she won't leave me alone like I'd prefer, but what if she says something to Dad that tells him I was at the beach when the boy was injured? I should have pretended to be sick instead of just coming along. Stomach flu probably would have worked.

I watch my father's jaw clench before he turns to Lenora. Annoyance and something that looks a little like discomfort passes across his face. Right now, it seems like Mayor Morgan is the one that wishes he could scurry away, not that I could ever picture him scurrying anywhere.

"Lenora, what are you doing here?" my dad says.

Curious, my own fears blow away on the non-existent wind. I blink, looking between the two. While my father looks like he wishes the woman in front of him would fall into a sinkhole, she looks both insane and pleased. Maybe now is the time to slip away.

No. I need to stay close to keep her from giving away my secrets. I'm stuck here.

"I was led to believe that this banquet was open to anyone who could afford a ticket. That would be me. I wanted to see you two together."

Dad casts a glance my way that promises we've added to the things we need to discuss. "You know Naomi?"

"Yes. She came to my shop the other day to look around for a jewelry box."

Once again, the scale feels warm against my skin. "I was looking for something to store my seashells and thought her shop would hold something more interesting."

Lenora cocks her head to the side, regarding me with a smug smirk that sends chills over me. "Yes. She bought one of my best jewelry boxes. I happened to see her earlier today as well."

Her pause makes me stiffen further. When Dad looks my way again, I force another smile. He asks, "Where?"

My teeth hurt with the grinding they now deal with. Lenora glances at me, a look that I can almost read as asking me if I want to tell him the truth, or maybe threatening to do so. A lump forms in my throat, and I worry that I'm going to start coughing. My eyes plead with her to not tell him of our last conversation.

With a smile that reminds me I'm at her mercy, the woman looks back at my father. "I was going for a walk in town. She was as well, and we ran into each other. I asked after the box she bought and was sad when she said that she... lost it. Did you get the replacement I sent, dear?"

I clear my throat to dislodge the lump. In the end, I need to try to talk around it, so my voice feels weak. "Yes, I did. Thank you."

"Try not to *lose* this one, dear. I must say, Mayor Morgan, Naomi looks nothing like you. Even without the bright red hair and blue eyes, she'd be the spitting image of your latest wife. Youngest then?"

Dad's lip lifts in a way that looks like the beginning of a snarl, but he checks it before it can be overly noticeable. "I don't see how my personal business is a concern."

She laughs, a chilling sound that I can't shake. "You're the mayor. Your business is everyone's. I can take a hint. I'll see you later."

Lenora saunters away. Dad turns to me. "I don't want you to have anything to do with that wretched woman."

My stomach feels sour. "I don't want to either. After our last conversation, I decided that I don't want to ever see her again. It seems that choice was taken from me."

"Don't be accepting her gifts either."

The scale burns more under my bodice as I prepare a lie. "It was only the box. I tossed it in the trash as I walked out tonight. I don't want to owe her anything."

"Good. She is not someone to trust. The fact that you're on her radar makes me nervous. Tell the driver to take you home. I'll tell everyone that the dinner didn't agree with you, which shouldn't be hard with the look on your face right now."

My mouth drops open at his over dramatic exaggeration of the situation. Surely Lenora isn't worth this sort of reaction. She's weird and creepy, but this is a bit much. Before I can argue, I take a look around. I wanted an excuse to leave. Arguing against his orders will not be smart. Nodding, I look my best at feeling sick, nod to a few people without answering their questions, and slip into the cool night. I ignore the lovely sounds of the ocean and find the driver for our limo.

As I walk across my room, I shed jewelry and clothing, leaving a trail on the floor. The party was exhausting enough, but Lenora's appearance made it worse. For once, the house is quiet. The only thing left is my scale necklace when I enter the bathroom. I rub it between my fingers, feeling the warm smoothness. While I do, I swear I feel it growing warmer.

The world spins, and I drop the scale to hang on my chest, ignoring the burning sensation that comes with it. I stumble and blink. My lungs stop working again, chest growing tight. Each attempt to breathe constricts it more. I try to suck in deep breaths, but no oxygen enters my system. My gasp sticks in my throat.

Last time, water helped, so I run over to my sink. Like before, the water eases my panic a little but not enough. I look toward the tub again. Despite my obvious distress, I notice something in the mirror. When I turn my face back to the reflective surface, I see long, needle-like teeth replacing my perfectly aligned mouthful. I gain enough air to scream, stepping back. One foot gets in the way of the other, making me fall while still mostly breathless. Pain blossoms in my head, and the world goes black.

Chapter Eight
Hallucinations

Gasping for breath, I surface in the tumultuous sea. Saltwater fills my mouth, and I cough and sputter. I try to move my arms and legs to bring me closer to shore, but it shrinks instead of coming closer. I cry in frustration and hopelessness as the next wave crashes over my head, my tears disappearing into the salty sea.

Screaming only fills my mouth with more water that I can't expel. My body flips and twists with the currents caused by the angry ocean. I think I'm still crying; it's too hard to tell when I'm covered by salty liquid. Is the burning from tears or the sea?

My feet strain for any hint of the bottom but find a great nothingness with no hint of solidness. When I feel like I can't hold my breath any longer, my head breaks the surface again. Coughing, I bob up and down in the water while struggling to stay up. The body of the dog under the pier floats over to me. In horror, I find myself sinking again.

Desperate fingers grasp the fur on the waterlogged corpse of someone's pet. I use it to find the surface again. I feel something hit me from behind, and I turn to find a severed leg. The jagged edge turns the dark water around me a bright red. I cry out and try to move away. Another wave hits me, plunging me back down into the darkness.

At this point, I consider giving up. I should give myself to the body of water I've almost worshiped my entire life. With that thought, my limbs stop moving. Peace settles over me. This is where I belong. I need to stop struggling.

My body hitting something hard breaks me from my acceptance. I find myself pushed across the sand on shore by the rolling waves. I open my eyes to see a dark sky above. Trying to take a deep breath of relief, I realize I still can't breathe.

Standing, I notice the sea pulling away from me, the distance between my toes and the edge of the water increasing quickly. I accepted it, and it rejected me. Tears roll down my cheeks as I chase after the water while holding my throat. I gasp for air, but none enters my lungs. The edges of my vision go dark while my limbs start to tingle.

My body grows weak without oxygen. Even now, the ocean flees from my presence. Despite my desire to reach the shore not long ago, the sight makes me want to scream and plead. I'd sob if I could inhale enough air to do so. I chase the retreating water, desperate to return to where I feel I belong. If I can't breathe either way, I need to be there.

It's too far. I can't catch it. Hopelessness consumes me, bringing me to my knees as my ability to see disappears. I fall onto the sand.

Crying out, I jerk awake. My head spins as I pull it off the cool tile. Wiping the drool from my face, I wince at the sound of murmurs through the outer wall. A thump and laughter makes me jump, which doesn't help my aching head. With a few blinks to clear my fogging vision, I straighten into a sitting position and take some time to breathe.

Once again, I wake in the bathroom. Clarity returns with a reminder of what happened last night. I want to jump to my feet in a hurry, but instead, I lean forward to get my hands and knees under me with a groan. For a moment, I stay in this position while queasiness churns in my stomach. Reaching up, I grab the edge of the sink and use it as leverage to get my feet under me. Standing makes the room spin faster.

With a gasp, I squeeze my eyes shut and press my hands against my temples. My stomach lurches, but I force it to behave as I sway back and forth. A few more moments like this are all I need to test opening my eyes again. Light-headedness causes a slight stumble.

The mirror hangs before me. Scared, I take a few more breaths before opening my mouth. My perfectly straightened teeth gleam in the light emitting from the bulbs over the mirror. Leaning closer, I open wider to make sure all is normal. I sigh in relief.

Recognition in my memory carries my feet to the cabinet holding my new box. Even with my heart broken over the loss of everything in my last treasure chest, I'm glad there isn't as much to sort through. I pull out the mysterious tooth I found a while back and hold it up close to my lips. My lips pull back, and my mind places what I'm looking at in place of my normal teeth. Grimacing, I drop my hand and look away.

It must have been a strange hallucination. With everything going on, it hasn't gone over my head that it all started when I found the tooth and scale. Not that I believe they have anything to do with the craziness happening to me. It's simply a coincidence.

That doesn't stop my mind from making the connection and throwing strange thoughts and visions into my head when the stress gets to be too much. Rubbing my eyes hurts, but I do it anyway, careful of the pointy object in my fingers. A knock sounds on my door, so I hurry to put the tooth back, hide the box back in its spot, and grab a robe.

Outside my bathroom, I trip over my dress, then over my shoes. Grumbling, I try to make my way to the door before the next knock and without falling on my face. I don't think my head could take another hit.

When I swing open the door, I find Clara on the other side. She looks in and gasps before jarring me to push past. "Why would you treat such an elegant and expensive dress like this? I need to get it cleaned, but it still doesn't deserve this type of disrespect. You need to learn how to treat your clothes properly. Not that your clothes are usually worth much."

I bite my tongue to keep from saying something nasty about the falsity of the look she's created. I've always been envious of her confidence, but that doesn't mean I want to care more about my appearance than anything else. Still, it would be rude to say.

Instead, I say the first thing that comes to mind to get her the hell out of my room. "You know why I had to leave early, right?"

She pauses, her fingers looped through the shoes still on the carpet. A grimace tells me she does when she looks back up at me. So worried about appearances that she forgot about my illness; fictional or not. There's no doubt in my mind she believes it to be a flaw in my character and not bad food.

As expected, she assumes I'm contagious instead of poisoned. "Why did you let me close to you if you could get me sick? Why are you always so dangerous to be around? This is ridiculous. You don't belong in this family with how weak you are."

I flinch at her harsh evaluation but say nothing, hoping she'll hurry herself out now. Clara's delicate hands shoo me away from the door. Part of me wants to pretend to cough on her during her exit, but I leave it be. Anything to get her out of here. She takes the dress with her.

As soon as she's gone, I decide a shower is necessary to wash off waking on the bathroom floor and Clara's words. I'm not weak. Am I? I am the only one that seems bothered by Father's treatment of us. Maybe that's more weakness than strength. Everyone else copes while I complain. The corner of my lip twists with the implication.

Even the water running over me can't settle my nerves. Clara says I'm weak, and she might just be right. I'm having strange moments that make me worry about my health. I've woken on the bathroom floor twice, this time after having a hallucination. Maybe I do need to be looked at.

As I climb out, a spot on my tile makes me look closer. I use a wet rag to find out it's blood. My shower was a distracted one while lost in my thoughts, so I probe the back of my skull with my fingers. Right in the center feels slightly tender. I gingerly prod it.

Pain shoots through my head. The world spins, and I need to grab the sink to keep from falling and making it worse. I suck in a sharp breath. Between the blood and the lump on my head, I think there is no question on whether I need to see someone or not. I throw on a pair of shorts and a tank top without looking before calling the doctor. They can get me in later this morning.

I have a few hours to kill. My grumbling stomach gives me a way to pass some of the time. I step around Abigail and Arabella arguing about shampoo before I reach the stairs. Worried about possible sudden dizziness, I take each step carefully. Lucy is at the table with her books and computer again. She barely acknowledges me with her forehead wrinkled in intense concentration. I try to be as quiet as possible.

When I reach the door to the kitchen, I hear Abigail scream in rage. A few small thumps bounce down the stairs. Arabella yelling about the expense being wasted makes me think it has to do with their argument. The sound is probably shampoo bottles tumbling down the stairs.

Lucy jumps, sighs with exasperation, and drops her head into her hands. To avoid making it worse, I slip into the kitchen. I see Brooke out the window that faces the front yard, sliding into the usual cloud of smoke billowing out an open car door. No one is in the kitchen or visible from the windows on the other two sides.

As usual, muffins, donuts, and fruit litter the counters. I bite my lip with indecision. Nothing seems worthy right now, not even my usual favorites, so I move to the fridge. My eyes fall on a small pack of shrimp. I tap the door and think with the corner of my lip beneath my teeth. Despite my fatigue, I feel the desire to make something this morning.

I pull out some eggs, cheese, and the shrimp. My hands hover over the mushrooms and peppers for a few moments before I pull them away. Not even the mushrooms seem appetizing to me, and I used to love them. I saute the shrimp first, then add scrambled eggs over top. I finish it off with a layer of cheese over everything. I can't flip omelets right, so I tend to just make scrambled eggs with goodies in them.

The fresh air hits me as soon as I'm out the door. I find a chair on the deck and plop down. Putting a bite in my mouth, I moan in pleasure. I'm not sure where this shrimp has been coming from, but it's been delicious every time we've had it. Not that I didn't like shrimp before. This is just the best shrimp I've ever had.

While I consume breakfast, I consider my options. I could call a cab or rideshare to go to my appointment, but I hate getting in strangers' cars alone. It doesn't matter if they've passed the necessary background checks or not. Looks like I'm walking.

Not that I mind. I love walking, and the air is warm but not hot. The sun hides behind harmless white clouds. A walk to clear my head on the way in will be perfect.

I take my last bite and feel at peace with the thought of a little exercise. I wash up the dishes I made and look for something else to occupy me for the next thirty minutes. It's a decent walk, so I'll need to leave then. I'd be lying if I said I didn't feel apprehensive about this appointment.

Chapter Nine
Strange Appetite

The needle enters my skin again, making me grit my teeth to keep the threatening hiss down. With the anesthetic, it doesn't exactly hurt. That doesn't mean it's a pleasant feeling. The smell of antiseptic is strong in my nostrils. Sneezing is not in my best interest right now, so I wiggle my nose to dispel the impending burst. I hope she finishes soon.

As soon as she's done, I let it loose. She says, "Bless you."

"Thanks," I say, rubbing my nose. "Are you sure there isn't a concussion? I felt terrible when I woke up on the bathroom floor this morning."

"As far as I can tell, you're all clear. Besides, this isn't as bad as it could be. I'm more worried about these hallucinations you speak of. They started before the first time you passed out?"

"No. I mean, I don't think so. I didn't feel quite right before the first time."

"Not right how?"

It takes a moment to put my thoughts in order. So much has happened in the last few days that it all blurs together. "I felt a sense of foreboding and didn't want most of the food on the table. Only the meat and shrimp tasted right. Later, I felt really thirsty and couldn't breathe. What's really strange is that running water over my face helped. Then I passed out."

"Maybe you were severely dehydrated."

"I don't think so. I drink plenty of water."

The doctor writes her notes on her pad and stares at it for a few seconds. "You couldn't breathe the second time?"

"Right. That's when I hallucinated those weird teeth."

"These are really strange symptoms, Naomi."

She doesn't have to tell me that. I've been wracking my brain for an explanation for longer than she has. I keep those thoughts in my head as she pores over her notes. I twist my fingers together, licking my lips and looking around the room.

Her voice brings my attention back. "Well, we are going to start simple and tackle the symptoms as best we can. Your vitals are all perfect, so I want to run some blood. I'd like to schedule an MRI as well."

"Okay."

"I'll have a nurse come in to draw some blood and put the order in for the MRI. The blood work won't take long. The hospital will call to schedule the scan. If anything else happens, please come back in. We need to figure this out."

Nodding, I kick my feet in the air while she walks out. When my butt starts to numb, I place my hands on the table and try to shift my rear end. The paper sticks to the back of my legs and makes me uncomfortable. I stand to free myself, ripping the paper in the process.

That's when the nurse decides to walk in. I notice her lips pursing, and I blush. "I accidentally tore the paper."

She smiles. "That's quite alright. Let me fix it for you because it's easiest for me if you're on the table."

The nurse sets her tray of needles and vials on the counter, tears off the ripped paper, and pulls down more. I climb back up and settle in for this part. I'm not a fan of needles, but I can't say I'm afraid of them. More of a discomfort than fear.

"Does it matter which arm?" she asks.

I shake my head. She wraps the band around my biceps and pulls it so tight I feel like my skin is going to split from the pressure. Gritting my teeth, I keep my lips pressed tight. After some poking and prodding, she sticks the needle in my arm. I'm happy to see she got it on the first try.

As soon as the band is off my arm, I let out a breath of relief and relax. Three full vials go into the cart. She reaches over and grabs a paper to hand to me.

"This is the hospital's scheduling number. You should hear from them in a few days. If not, you can try calling," the nurse says. "I took the liberty of scheduling your follow up. If the date and time don't work for you, talk to the receptionist."

"Thank you."

With one last smile, she opens the door and walks out. I jump off the table, pulling the paper with my thighs again. I hate this stuff. Outside, I stop and enjoy the warm sunshine. A slight tingle pulls my attention to where the nurse took my blood. Curious, I pull the medical tape and gauze off.

That nurse is good. No bruise. I can't even see the usual pinprick to tell me exactly where the needle went in. Wrapping the gauze in the tape, I toss it into a nearby trash can. I pause to consider.

There is enough allowance left in my account for a lunch out. I don't feel like returning to the turmoil of home, so that seems to be the best bet for me. Turning toward the boardwalk, I make my way in that direction. The crowds close in around me as soon as my feet hit the rough path. I keep my mind away from the sand and move toward the end of the boardwalk that is furthest from town hall.

I'm technically not on the beach right now, so he can't yell at me over it. That doesn't mean he won't anyway if he sees me. A few new signboards warn of possible shark activity in the area. My mind returns to the poor boy who is now missing a leg. I hope it was simply a shark.

Shaking my head, I wonder what's wrong with me. The poor boy has to live the rest of his life with one leg. Life will be infinitely harder now than it used to be for him. Yet, all I can think is that I hope it was just a shark.

What else would it be? The leg was bitten right off. Guilt tickles my senses with the thought that I was more worried about what's in the water than what it did to its victim. A teenager's life is ruined. It's not like I'm going to go into the water. The only thing I should be hoping for is that it doesn't happen to anyone else.

A delicious scent grabs my attention and pulls me from my dark thoughts. My feet stop in front of a building, and I turn to take a deep inhale. Seafood. I've spent my entire life living in a beach town, so seafood is an expected. I've never craved it as I have lately though. Maybe I should have mentioned to the doctor that my tastes have changed, not just the weird flavors at supper. I've been noticing it a lot lately.

With a shrug, I walk into the small restaurant that is made to look like a ship. Ship wheels hang on the walls with nets and sea junk. I make my way to the counter and order a fish sandwich, sitting down at one of the round wooden tables. My food comes out within minutes.

Cautious, I take a bite of a fry. It doesn't taste bad like I was afraid it would, but it also isn't as good as it should be. I used to love fries. The greasy potatoes always hit the spot. Some sort of weird dip sits on the edge of my fish-shaped plate, right at the tip of the tail. Dipping the rest of the fry in it, I bring the next bite to my mouth.

It's some sort of crab dip, and it's delicious. I eat half my fries, smothered in this special sauce, with no desire to finish the rest when the small cup is empty. The fish sandwich goes down much easier. Cod, I'd say.

Before I know it, I'm staring at empty hands and wishing there was more fish. I ate that so fast that I have no idea if I chewed it or not. Frowning, I throw my napkin on the plate, deposit the trash in the appropriate bin, and step out into the brine-filled air.

It seems that the doctor is focusing on my blood and head. Maybe she should have run some tests on my stomach. I'm like a bottomless pit for meat and seafood but not all that hungry for anything else. Something has to be up with my digestive system.

I'm too unsettled to head home and deal with my sisters, so I find my feet sinking in the sand after turning my phone off. I usually don't bring it to the beach because of the GPS apps Dad likes to install on them. I didn't think I'd end up here. This far away, there isn't as much of a chance of running into my father, but I'm still careful to scan my surroundings. I'm almost at the end of the boardwalk, so the crowd is light here.

A few surfers ignore the shark warnings, riding the waves into the beach. I feel a little envious over the freedom they must feel on the waves. Sighing, I walk over to where the sand becomes impeded by rocks and settle down. The crowd falls away far enough that I feel safe to sing.

The song flows, if not loud enough to be heard far. Anxiety washes away on the words. I close my eyes and remember my mother's hand in mine as she used to sing along with me. Tears sting behind my eyes, provoked by mournful memories after days of uncertainty. One escapes and trickles down my cheek.

I hear a splash near my perch and stop singing. As I open my eyes, I search the water in front of me. The greenish glimmer catches my attention again. My teeth clench.

What is the chance some sea creature followed me from a couple of miles down the beach? Is this just another hallucination? Sharks don't shine in the water like this. Something sparkly is catching the light of the sun and throwing it back to the surface bright enough to be noticed. I didn't see it when I closed my eyes.

I'm not sure how long I sit and stare, but the colored patch in the moving water doesn't change. Maybe it's some kind of trash at the bottom. My hand finds the scale under my shirt, pulling it out to compare the colors I see in the water to what hangs from the shells on my neck. Same bluish green.

A new sound pulls my eyes away from my query. A dolphin pod swims out in the waves. When I look back at the shimmering patch, I see it moving toward the swimming animals. I climb to my feet, careful on the slick rocks.

"Move, dolphins. Please move," I whisper.

My heart stops when I lose the shiny spot in the deeper water. The dolphins seem to sense no danger, so I feel stupid to be worried. As my breath slowly comes back, one of the dolphins lets out a pained cry.

Tears fall down my cheeks as I watch the others either swim away or turn on whatever is attacking them. My fists clench at my side, and my teeth find my bottom lip. A large splash makes me jump, bringing the taste of blood to my teeth, so I stop biting my lip.

The next wave is blood red, causing me to take a step back. A large tail fin from some kind of fish breaks the surface before disappearing again. I turn to hurry away. At least, that's my intention.

Slipping, my foot twists as it slides between two large rocks. Pain shoots up my leg, and I yell through grit teeth. The sounds in the water behind me stop, so I turn my head to look. The fight is over, but a large shadow moves toward the beach.

Frantic, I try to pull my foot out but only twist it more. I whimper, the tears streaming down my face unchecked. Closing my eyes, I take a deep breath to try to calm myself. When I open them again, I look back to see the shape halfway to the beach with a hint of color, a trail of dark red lingering behind it.

Bending, I grab my ankle with my hands and find the way of least resistance to position my foot. I'm able to pull it out without much more trouble, clenching my jaw to the pain. As I hurry toward the boardwalk with a limp, I refuse to look back.

My feet take me into the crowd, and I finally feel safe enough to turn around. The water is smooth. No glimmer or shadows mar the surface. My eyes search for a little longer before I hurry home on a twisted ankle.

Chapter Ten
Poison

The walk home took hours because I was unwilling to call for help. Any of my sisters would have expected repayment of their choice. Who knows what that could end up meaning? Father would have asked too many questions, even if I called him blocks from the sand. Ride sharing isn't smart with my recent splurges. Not that I feel safe doing that alone. I've heard too many stories.

Therefore, the dining room light is the brightest in the house as I hobble up the steps to the front door. Instead of entering, I take a few moments to lean against the door. I breathe, trying to will away the agony that is my throbbing ankle. I'm pretty sure my foot is numb at this point as well. Not the areas above it.

The door opens, and I find myself stumbling into the house, trying with everything that I have to keep on my feet. There's no way I'd be able to get back up once I'm down. Emma reaches out and tries to steady me, concern shining in her brown eyes. Her blonde ponytail swings back and forth as she dips with me. Thanks to her, I don't fall.

The stumble didn't feel good at all. I take deep breaths in and out through my teeth while waiting for the throbbing to settle down. The stairs are going to be pure torture, but sleeping anywhere else isn't an option.

"Are you alright, Naomi?" Emma asks.

"I took a walk and twisted my ankle. It's been a hard trip home."

"Want help to the dining room?"

The thought of dealing with this pain and trying to smile through it while everyone else bickers isn't on my to-do list. Father would also possibly berate me more because we haven't spoken since the banquet.

I shake my head. "I don't have much of an appetite. I just want a long bath and rest right now."

"Are you sure? Maybe you should go to the hospital?"

"No. It's just bad because I've been walking on it. The inflammation will die down with some rest. If it doesn't by tomorrow morning, I'll let you know."

"Then you'll let me take you?"

I nod. "Go back to the meal."

"I was just going out to collect something Clara left in the yard. She can wait. Let me help you up the stairs." Protests don't help, so I allow Emma to place her shoulder under my arm and half carry me up the stairs.

When we make it into my room, I motion at my bed. "Drop me here. I need to rest and can do everything else myself. Thank you for the help."

"Are you sure?"

"Yes. Don't forget Clara's whatever. You know the tantrum she'll throw. I'll be fine, so enjoy dinner."

Emma slips out and gently closes the door. After a few minutes, I limp into my bathroom and start the water in the tub with some lavender bubbles. I put my towel and washcloth close, then sit on the toilet lid and breathe through the fresh waves of agony brought on by all my movement. Getting my shoes off will be difficult and unpleasant, so I wait until I'm as naked as I can be before getting to that. My shirt and bra fly toward the wicker hamper in the corner.

I stare at my shoes, glad I wore sneakers this time to add support to my ankle. The strings come loose easily, but removing the shoe from the bad foot leaves me making my lip bleed again. I sit and moan for a bit. The sock is much easier. The sight greeting me makes me wince with a hiss.

I'm not sure how my foot even fits in my shoe to begin with. It's so swollen that I can understand why it's numb. I really should not have walked the whole way home. I hope I didn't screw it up worse. My sock left a nasty crease in my inflamed ankle, which only adds to the pain.

By the time I'm done with this struggle, I have to hop hurriedly over to turn off the water. I slide in, letting the heat take some of the muscle ache. It does nothing for the ankle, but all my other muscles are stiff and clenched from the long, awkward walk home through tight pain. At least, I can find relief from one part of my misery.

My door shuts outside my bathroom. I can't see through this closed wood, so I freeze and wonder what's going on. Footsteps move through my private space. I hope no one comes in here.

A soft tap is followed by Emma's voice. "Naomi? Are you alright?"

"I'm fine. Can't say it was easy, but I feel better already."

"Okay. Do you have your phone?"

I look over at the bathroom sink where I left it. It's a bit of a reach, one I'm not willing to try with a bum ankle. She doesn't need to know that. "Yeah."

"I brought a heat pack and ice pack in my backpack coolers, separate, of course. Try alternating them. I also brought your water thermos and some painkillers. If you need anything else, text me."

Having one caring sister makes my throat almost close up. "I will. Thank you. I mean it, Emma. I really appreciate it."

"No worries. I'll check on you in the morning to see if you need the hospital. Unless you need me, goodnight."

"Goodnight."

I wait until I hear the outside door open and close again before sinking further into my bubbles. The scale around my neck bobs on top. Staring at it, I can't help but remember the glimmer in the sea being the same color. That thought causes me to shiver in the hot water. Should I still be wearing this thing? It came from some nasty and dangerous thing that crippled a teen and I can only imagine what else.

The frantic cries of the dolphins pierce my ears. Covering them does no good because the noise is in my head. Frothy red water made those waves. What could do that to a dolphin? Shark? I'm sure they could, but it happened so fast. I know nothing about sharks besides the joy of collecting their teeth off the beach.

My leg itches, and I reach down to give it a quick scratch before returning to my contemplation. Ever since I first saw the shine in the water, my life has been creepy and uncertain. Dead animals. Weird hallucinations. Strange appetites. Maimed boys. What could it all mean? Why is this happening to me?

I have to pause to give my other leg a more aggressive scratch. Lifting the floating scale over my head, I run my finger over it again. There's no way this thing is magic. Lenora can't be right, can she? No. There's absolutely no way anything she said is real. I'm simply stretching for things to explain something that seems unexplainable but probably isn't. Logic will answer what's going on. Maybe it's just plain bad luck.

"Oh my God! Stop itching!"

The scale falls on top of my bubbles as I take the time to scratch with both hands. All ten fingers strain to relieve the annoyance. The scale does that weird color shift I've seen during only a couple other experiences. When the skin under my fingers feels rough, I pull them back.

Did I catch some disease when I hurt myself? Did I scratch too deep? I stare at the bubbles a little longer while deciding what to do, almost too scared to look with all the recent strangeness. I need to know what's going on.

I push the bubbles away, only to have them cover the space I made within seconds. The itching returns with a vengeance, which makes me squirm enough to hurt my ankle more. Giving up, I lift my leg straight up. My mouth opens to scream, but nothing comes out.

The skin on my legs is covered with scale-like marks that gleam a purplish blue. They're fading before my eyes, but I know what I see. I try to scream again. My voice is no longer working. Then comes the feeling of drowning.

I don't understand the new feeling either. Yes, I'm in water. No, my face is not below the surface. How can I be drowning? My lungs constrict as if to tell me that my objections carry no weight. Gripping the sides of the tub, I try to heave myself out. My foot jars on the bottom, and I open my mouth in another soundless yell.

Water covers my face. For a moment, I can breathe, which makes absolutely no sense whatsoever. It only lasts for a moment, then I find myself choking on warm, soapy liquid. I pull myself above the surface and cough, happy to hear sound escaping me again.

With both hands on the side of the tub, I heave myself up and over, gasping for life-giving oxygen. My palms slip on the ceramic and spill me to the floor. My bad foot hits the faucet, making tears roll down my cheeks. Curling into a ball, I sob away the pain until I can bear it.

Grasping fingers reach for the towel, finding it after a few seconds. I pull myself into a sitting position and wrap the fluff around me as if my life depends on it. What the hell just happened? That had to be another hallucination. Right?

Of course, that's what it was. There's no way something like that can be real. Maybe Lenora laced that necklace with some kind of hallucinogen. That will show in my blood. It has to. Doesn't it?

The uncertainty is killing me, but I don't see any way of becoming certain about any of this. My life has been confusing and impossible. Ever since I found that scale, nothing has been right; I haven't been myself. It must be that scale, and there's no way I'll ever believe mermaids are real or that magic exists. Those are the fancies of an unsettled mind. I stopped believing in mermaids around the same time I learned unicorns and dragons aren't real either.

Lenora is messing with me. That's what this is. She has some kind of vendetta against my father, as I saw at the banquet, and is using me to enact it. There is no other explanation that makes sense. Either that, or I'm going insane. That's another possibility. Maybe my MRI will verify that.

After spending a few more minutes calming myself with logic that doesn't make sense, I use my hands to slide closer to the tub. I reach in to pull the plug, needing to pull myself up a bit to get a firm grasp on it. Something touches my fingers, and I jerk my hand out, the scale necklace flying across the bathroom and landing behind the toilet.

With everything going on, I no longer trust it. If Lenora did something to it, who knows what will happen with continued contact. It's best to not touch it more than necessary. I wonder if it's the necklace or scale. I trust neither nearly as much as I trust that woman, which isn't at all. It can stay there for as long as needed. It might be important if my blood comes back saying I was drugged. Evidence.

Climbing to my feet is as difficult as I predicted it would be earlier. After a few tries, lots of breathing, and a little whimpering, I find myself limping back to my bed. Dressing brings a whole new agony. I decide a nightgown is better than pants.

Once I'm settled in, I take the time to examine my legs again. Nothing bizarre meets my gaze or my searching fingers. Whatever had startled me so badly in the tub is gone. This only confirms that it was a hallucination. Whatever is causing this is playing my thoughts and wonderings against me. That's all it is.

I don't have sharp teeth. I'm not drowning in the air. Scales aren't growing out of my legs. My teeth are normal. There is absolutely nothing abnormal about me. The doctor will get to the bottom of all this strangeness.

Satisfied, I grab the ice pack Emma brought me. I just soaked in heat, so ice is probably the way to go now. I settle in and try to ignore the throbbing in my ankle. Blood results come back tomorrow. I'll have my answers then.

Chapter Eleven
Fanatics

Sunshine in my window brings wakefulness. Once again, I have slept too long to make my morning trip. After what happened yesterday, do I really want to? I'm not sure what was in the water, but I know I don't want to find out. Although, I can't let this strangeness take away my one freedom.

The ocean calls to me. I want to walk along the shore before the sun is up all the way. I want to feel the sand between my toes and pick up little treasures. Most of all, I want to raise my voice and give tribute to the loved one lost with our special song. Fear can't be allowed to destroy my one small sliver of peace.

It's kind of hard to get up early enough to slip out unnoticed when I'm either passed out on the floor or in too much pain to get any sleep. That thought brings the fact that the agony is gone to my cluttered mind. Flipping the covers back, I look at my ankle and foot in amazement. There is absolutely no swelling, no pain. This is strange.

I take the time to gently feel the sore spot on my scalp. Fingers touch the stitches, but I feel no sourness. Maybe my painkillers are still working.

Emma chooses this moment to knock on my door and softly call my name. I tell her to come in while I swing my feet over the side of the bed. She opens the door as I gingerly put weight on my ankle. It doesn't hurt.

"Guess you don't need the hospital after all," Emma says.

"Seems not."

"I was expecting to need to take you with how badly you were walking last night."

I nod and continue to look at my feet. "To be fair, I fully expected you to as well. I don't understand it. I could barely get my shoe off because of the swelling last night."

"Maybe it was the fact that you kept walking on it?"

"That's the only thing I can think of. I'm sorry I worried you. Here are your things back. Thank you so much for all the help. I really do appreciate it."

I gather everything she brought to help me and give it to her with a smile. She returns my smile and says, "Of course. I know things seem hard here, so at least one sister has to have your back. You'll tell me if you need help later?"

"I will. Promise."

"I suggest you stay in for today. There is supposed to be another big storm moving in. Wouldn't want to aggravate your ankle, just in case."

"No, I'm not going anywhere. I think I need an easy day today."

Emma nods and walks out of the room. I watch the door close behind her with a sigh. This place never really feels like home, but I at least have one family member that can make it a little easier. What I said is true; I plan to stay inside today. My room will be my safe haven for now. I'll only leave for food and beg off eating dinner with everyone else.

First, I need a trip to the bathroom. I test my weight on my ankle again, wondering if maybe it was my panic exaggerating the pain. There's no way something that hurt that much can feel perfectly fine this morning. Emma is right. Just in case, I'll take it easy and rest today.

As I enter the bathroom, I see the glimmer of the scale behind the toilet. I use a piece of toilet paper to push it further behind to hide it from view. If there is poison on it, it will only contaminate my box. If not, then I'm wrong and as crazy as I think I am, making it completely safe to wear.

I do what I need, grab my phone off the sink and walk toward the door. Still, no pain, so I slowly let myself relax. It seems that I'm healed completely. When I reach the door into my bedroom, I pause and look back at the cabinet. My fingers drum against the frame while my teeth worry at my lip. Now is as good a time as any to do some research.

Walking over, I dig my treasure trove from beneath the towels and pull the strange tooth out from my meager collection. I really need to find more to put in it. My heart aches at the thought of my largest collection in a dumpster somewhere. It deserves a better home; *I* deserve a better home. Fueled by anger, I brush the tears away, shove the tooth into my pocket before hiding the box again, then leaving my room.

The quiet is eerie, and I wonder when the shouting is going to break out. No one is in the hall. I check the time on my phone and realize it's almost lunchtime. That would explain it. Everyone is most likely off on whatever errand or event for the day. I guess that's what happens when a throbbing ankle keeps you up all night.

Downstairs, I hear classical music coming from the living room. I glance in to see Emma painting on her easel. She glances over. "Do you need something?"

I shake my head. "Just seeing who is in here. I'm going to grab something to eat and take it to my room, then do nothing important. I haven't done that in a while."

"Good. Everyone deserves an easy day. I mean it though. If you need me, I'm only a text away. No one else is here today."

"Will do. Do you want anything from the kitchen?"

"Already ate, but thank you."

Nodding, I make my way through the empty dining room and into the kitchen. I make a turkey sandwich, fill up another thermos of water, and grab a sweet tea. So I don't need to come back down when everyone else is here, I grab a box of crackers and the spray cheese that Arabella and Clara turn their noses up at.

Back in my room, I grab my laptop, sit it on my nightstand, and drop myself onto my bed to eat my sandwich. As soon as I'm done, I put the computer in my lap and flip the top open. I place the tooth right below the screen while it starts up. I tap the edges.

"What do I even search for?" I mutter.

Shrugging, I type in *strange shark's tooth* and hit search. I have to start somewhere. Nothing comes that looks even remotely similar to what I have sitting right in front of me. This may be a monumental task I'm not well equipped for. Lucy would be able to tell me how best to search for something like this—all the research she has to do for school—but I don't want to bother her studies. Emma might just ask more questions. Everyone else would only laugh.

I'm on my own. I search for ocean creatures with sharp teeth, horrified at all the creepiness that comes up on my screen. The closest I find is the angler fish, but that's not right either. This tooth is too big for that, unless some giant species lives somewhere. Most of the ocean still remains unexplored, so I can't help but wonder if this is some new animal forced to come from the deep for some reason.

Traitor fingers start typing something else, but I delete it before I complete the word. I will not search that and give voice to the doubts and insanity threatening me. Huffing, I sit the laptop beside me to avoid the temptation. I can think of nothing else to search for because I'm terrible at this kind of thing.

Instead of driving myself crazier with questions and stupid searches, I pick up my horror novel. I still have a quarter of the book left, so I might as well use my self-imposed downtime to finish it. Only I can't focus. This is ridiculous.

Grabbing my laptop again, I type *mermaids* in the search bar. Proving to myself that it's not possible is the best way to get my mind to shut up about it. Pictures and articles of half human women with fishtails smile back at me from my screen. I grimace because this is no happy fairytale I'm dealing with right now. This is ridiculous.

My skepticism nearly makes me shut down my computer, but just to get the annoyance out, I type *Are mermaids real* into the search. Once again, I'm assaulted by smiling fake pictures. A site comes up that allows you to record a mermaid sighting. I laugh but click on it anyway.

So many fantastic tales of fishy encounters fill my eyes. Some swear that they saw one. Others say something that felt like it had arms saved them from drowning, which doesn't sound at all like what I'm experiencing. Not enough violence. The few with pictures are either too blurry or far away to make out, or they are clearly a dolphin, shark, or large fish.

People will find any excuse to make it seem like their fantasies are real. I can't blame them. Life can be bland or traumatic. It's easier to believe in myths and magic than it is to live in the real world that feels so dark and hopeless. It's easy to get lost in fiction to avoid reality. That's one of the reasons I read so much.

I hit the back button and scroll down further. I'm about to give up when something catches my eye. "The Real Mermaids," I whisper as I read.

I click on an article in the blog titled *This Isn't Ariel*. My eyes widen as I read on, so I start over and read aloud in hopes I'm misunderstanding things.

"Mermaids aren't the cuddly creatures that people think they are. They don't save lost travelers or lure lonely sailors to true love. They're predatory and dangerous, so don't be fooled by those that tell you otherwise. Here are some accounts of attacks blamed on something else and the evidence that mermaids are really behind it."

The next few paragraphs are shark attack incidents and accidents involving humans, wild creatures, and beloved pets. My mind goes over the dog and dolphins again, stopping when I remember the teenage boy that was dragged from the waves without one of his legs. This is crazy, which only makes me want to leave the site behind. The final paragraph saying the government knows and is using the attacks as experiments—and other conspiracies—increases the urge to roll my eyes.

I hover over the back button but don't click on it. Instead, I find myself going over the attacks again. Some evidence sounds made up, exaggerated, or actually points in the other direction. Still, some similarities keep me from running from the page and never returning. At the bottom, a contact sheet asks for links of possible attacks to be investigated. I bite my lip.

After some deliberation, I open a new tab and search for the news story of the boy that was attacked. I feel stupid doing this, but I copy the link, paste it in the form, and mark it anonymous. Clicking send is even harder than I expected it would be.

This all has to be fake. None of this is real. There has to be a real-world explanation for everything going on. Then this won't be proven as some mythical creature attack, right? I hit send.

Next, I browse the forums and get an idea after about an hour down the rabbit hole—or would that be whirlpool for this subject? I've already convinced myself that Lenora doesn't know anything she's talking about. Mermaids aren't real, and these people are all crazy.

But maybe someone in here is like me and can at least help me identify it.

"Damn it. I really am an idiot," I mutter.

I grab my phone to take a picture of the tooth, then walk into the bathroom to stick my phone behind the toilet. It takes a few tries to get a worthy picture of the scale, but I'm not touching it again. After I make an account, I upload the pictures on the forum with a short post.

I'm not sure I really believe in any of this, but I can't identify these. Can anyone tell me what they are? Mermaids can't be real. What are these really?

Maybe not the best message for a site full of fanatics, but maybe the right eyes will see it. To avoid doing anything else I'll be embarrassed about later, I shut my laptop off and decide on a snack. I place a cracker in my mouth and squirt some fake cheese in with it.

When my phone starts ringing, I find myself choking on cracker and cheese paste. I'm able to get it down and answer. "Hello?"

"Naomi Morgan?"

"Speaking."

"Are you alright?"

I force another swallow. "Sorry, I was choking on a cracker. I'm fine now."

"Well, be careful there. So, I'm calling about your blood work."

"You got the results?"

"Not exactly." What the hell is that supposed to mean? She doesn't leave me hanging. "There was some sort of contamination, so results were impossible to find."

"Contamination?"

"Some strange traces within your blood. Could have come from any number of things. The doctor would like you to redo the blood work. You can come in any time, and we will draw it and get you out of here as soon as possible."

I glance at the time. Still a couple of hours until they close. "Today alright?"

"That's fine, Ms. Morgan."

We say goodbye and hang up. So much for my peaceful afternoon. Oh well, I can use a little fresh air anyway. I need answers.

Chapter Twelve
Storms and Allies

"Why were you here for this?" Emma asks.

My eyes jerk away from my hands to land on my sister. Her blonde ponytail has a little paint mixed in with it, and there's a smudge of blue under her right eye. When I went to leave, others were home, and Emma was still painting in the living room. Of course, she saw me as I dodged Brooke barreling through the entryway. And, of course, she wanted to come.

"Why are you so nice to me?" I ask.

This question derails her curiosity. "What?"

"Everyone else in that house is just plain rotten to me. I get that all our sisters have different personalities, but you seem to be the only one that actually cares about the others. Lucy might. It's hard to tell through her caution and anxiety."

Emma laughs. "Well, if you count me and Lucy, I'd say three out of seven isn't bad."

"Three out of seven? That's two, not three."

"I'm counting you as well, Naomi."

My eyes widen. All I've been trying to do is survive in a house full of hostility. I never looked at it as me coming out as one of the good ones. There's so much going on that she doesn't know though. All my secrets make it feel like she's wrong.

I open my mouth to reply with some inadequate statement, but the door opens to admit my nurse with another tote full of vials and needles. "Let's see if we can make this work this time."

"What work this time?" Emma asks.

The nurse looks at me, and I choose to answer. "They took some blood yesterday. It was contaminated somehow, so they want to take more."

"That happens?"

"Sometimes," the nurse says with a shrug. "It could have been anything. A faulty vial. A contaminated needle. Even a clumsy lab tech. I'm sure this one will give us the answers we need."

"Answers for what?"

My nurse raises an eyebrow before cinching the band tight again. I wince and turn to Emma. "Remember when you thought I was acting weird and sick?"

"Yeah."

"Well, it happened again after the banquet. I had a minor hallucination and passed out on the bathroom floor again."

Emma widens her brown eyes, crinkling the area smeared with blue. "Really? I told you we should have gotten you checked out earlier."

"Well, I'm here now."

"You are."

Once my blood is taken, we walk out of the doctor's office. The sunlight has disappeared beneath a cover of thick clouds. Toward the sea, the sky only gets darker. "Looks like we need to get home."

"How about we get some food first?"

"Do you really think that's a good idea with the weather moving in? Storms come fast over the water."

"Yep. Everyone needs to eat. What are you in the mood for?"

"Seafood," I say without hesitation. My stomach goes for one thing and forgets all else when that question is asked.

"There's a decent one not far down the block. My treat. I have plenty of allowance left."

The restaurant is nice without being fancy. Pleasant music permeates the air, giving a calm environment. The pungent smell of fish penetrates my nostrils and makes my mouth water instantly. I take a deep breath, feeling my stomach rumble. Emma must hear it because she sends me a smug grin. Okay, eating was a good idea.

The hostess sits us at a table in the back. Most of the restaurant is empty. Sane people hunker down when a storm heads to town. We settle down at a table with a green tablecloth and take the menus. I take a sweet tea while Emma asks for water with lemon.

"So, want to tell me more about these episodes you're having? I didn't want to push in the doctor's office," Emma says without taking her eyes off the menu.

I look over the fish until I find a tuna steak that looks absolutely delicious. When I look back up, I find my sister regarding me with her hands folded over the menu. I'm not getting out of this.

With a sigh, I fold the list of food in front of me and lean back. "It's not more than what you already know. I felt off, couldn't breathe, then I looked in the mirror and saw sharp teeth in my mouth. After that, I blacked out."

"Is that all?"

I laugh. "That's not enough?"

"I just want to know everything. Maybe I can help."

"I don't think you can help with this. I'm hallucinating, craving seafood, seeing things that can't be real but are, and generally feel crazy."

"What things have you seen?"

I wince and look away, saved by the waitress' return to take our orders. Taking a sip of my drink, I avoid her gaze. How much will everything that's happened freak her out? For the first time in my life,

I feel like I have an ally. It's a strange feeling, one I like. I don't want to lose it, even if I'm not sure how to respond to this.

The waitress walks away, so Emma takes that as her cue to continue the conversation. "Naomi?"

I sigh. "You'll think I'm crazy."

"I won't."

"If Dad finds out..."

"I won't tell him."

Another sip of tea helps calm my nerves. Do I want to tell her? What's the point of having an ally if I don't utilize the benefits? If I lose her by telling her, was she ever truly an ally to begin with?

"I've made trips to the beach. I saw a boy that almost knocked me over have his leg ripped off in the ocean."

Her mouth drops. "You were there? Dad would be so angry. No, I'm not going to say anything. I like this secret pact. What happened? All I know is what the news says."

I shrug and take a break to swirl my straw. "I didn't see much. He was catching a football and almost knocked me into the water. I walked further down the beach to the pier, where I found a dead dog that looked half eaten and all rotten. When I came back, they were pulling him out of the water without one of his legs. There was so much blood."

"That's terrible. I'd have nightmares for days."

But I haven't. That's something to consider because most people would have bad dreams. I have bad memories, but my subconscious doesn't seem to want to replay it in my sleep. Maybe it's because half the time I'm passed out and not sleeping.

Instead of admitting that fault, I continue. "Yesterday, after I went to the doctor, I took another stroll but all the way to the other end of the beach."

"Away from our father?"

"As far away as possible. I sat on some rocks and saw something shimmering in the water. It was a shadow, but it shined a bluish-green color. Some dolphins were swimming out in the waves. I watched the shadow move out to them and killed one or more. That's when I twisted my ankle."

"That's strange. What do you think it was?"

I shake my head and look out the window. Water cascades down the glass that takes up most of the front of the building. Looks like the storm has started, which feels oddly appropriate for this moment.

How much can I tell Emma? She accepted my weird symptoms and my encounters well enough. What if I tell her about the tooth and scale? What if I tell her about Lenora? None of that sounds like a good idea. A new ally is a shaky one. I need to feel her out more. No talk of mermaids yet, or ever. My hand itches to check my email to see if I have any responses to my forum post. Even that feels stupid thinking about it.

"I have no idea," I say after a while. "I tried to research what might do this kind of thing, but I can't find anything more concrete than a shark."

That's not a lie. Mermaids aren't concrete. Mermaids are a bedtime story.

"Maybe that's all it is then," Emma says. "The colors you saw might have simply been the sun reflecting off the water."

I nod in agreement, feeling a huge relief to find our meals here. We can distract ourselves from this strange thought with food; delicious, mouth-watering food. I'm not sure what this weird new seafood addiction is, but I'm going to enjoy it while I can. If there's one thing this town has plenty of, it's seafood.

We let the conversation turn toward less threatening topics. I'm embarrassed to admit our sisters are less threatening. Together, we recount the stupidest arguments we've witnessed and the ones that ended in the most unexpected ways.

"Do you remember the time," Emma says, "when Clara took a pair of Brooke's pants without realizing they weren't washed and Brooke had accidentally walked through poison ivy?"

I snort. "She was itchy for weeks. I feel bad that I find that memory hilarious, but if anyone deserved that to happen, it's Clara."

"And she never learned her lesson."

"Not even close."

"I need to get better at finding ways to make her not want to take my stuff. Dealing with her thinking you're always contagious is so much better than needing to fight for your stuff back. You're my hero."

Laughter takes us long past the point where food is cleared from the table. When we finally stop reminiscing, the storm is fully underway. The thunder rolls hard enough to make the building shake. Lightning brightens the dark sky momentarily.

I frown. "Maybe we should wait it out."

The manager locks the door to keep others from coming in and lets most of his staff go. The wind throws leaves and twigs into the window. Sheltering in place seems to be a good idea.

"Nonsense. Locals know how to drive in this weather. I'll call for ride share. We'll stay dry, and Father won't send the cavalry out after us. He wouldn't be happy to have us missing overnight."

I clench my teeth and grimace. She's right. I'm already in a lot of trouble. The fact that I missed the last two dinners probably pours more hot water over me. Best to get home before things explode again. I hate being the target with an audience full of women who find it entertaining.

The desire for two different kinds of safety war within me. In the end, the risk of angering Father seems higher than falling into danger during the short ride home. It's out of my hands anyway. Either I leave with Emma, or I stay here when she goes. She's already using her phone to book the ride. At least I won't be alone with the strange driver. I'll wait and ride with her.

Even though my hands itch to check for responses, I don't bother. A very large part of me—humongous—wants nothing to do with the mermaid forums. It's the small nagging part of me that keeps begging me to look and see what people have to say to my pictures. I'll have plenty of time to look before bed.

The vehicle pulls up, a heavy-duty pickup with an extended cab. The remaining staff unlocks the door long enough to let us out. The wind hits me hard, rain stinging my skin where it pelts relentlessly. We climb in, and Emma gives him our address while I wipe the water from my eyes before buckling my seatbelt.

Of course, our driver recognizes the address and gives us an appraising look in the rearview as he presses the gas. "Mayor's daughters?"

"That clear?" I say with heavy sarcasm.

"I see you in newspapers and on news programs sometimes. You're like famous."

Emma laughs. "Thanks."

"No, I'm serious..."

The wind pushes the truck sideways, stopping his words more effectively than either of us could. As soon as he straightens the tires out again, it pushes us the other way. He hits a large puddle of water, and we hydroplane. Grasping the back of the front seat, I find myself screaming.

One pair of tires hits a high curb. The truck spins, and my screams escalate, joined by Emma's. Then the vehicle flips and rolls, right into the window of an ice cream shop. A table shatters the window, and the chair flies into the back seat. This time, my unconsciousness has a physical reason.

Chapter Thirteen
Painful Wakening

Beeping infiltrates the void I exist in first. Blinking, I try to force my eyes open without success. Soft murmurs sound as if from far away. The sharp tang of antiseptic and what smells like bandaids permeate my existence next. If I could scrunch my face in annoyance, I would. It feels impossible to move even the smallest muscle. I ache.

The distant voices gain more distance before the loud thump of a door closing pulls me the rest of the way out of my stupor. My eyes open slowly, closing repeatedly against the brightness they are unaccustomed to. After many tries, I'm able to squint enough to make out blurry surroundings. The door sounds again, and I hear the last voice I want to hear when I'm so disoriented.

"Naomi? You're awake?" My dad's voice has a hint of both worry and frustration in it. I'm sure the latter will take over the former as soon as I can handle waking fully.

I open my mouth to talk, dryness bringing on a harsh hacking. A plastic rim meets my lips, and I gulp greedily at the chemical tasting water that touches my tongue. The world slowly comes into focus to leave me looking at Travis Morgan placing the pink cup back on the little tray by my bed.

Even now, his brown hair looks impeccable. The worry turns to pure frustration with a mix of anger in his brown eyes. "What the hell were you thinking?"

My head tries to split open at his raised voice. A moan escapes me as I clutch my temples to try to hold my brain in my skull. I gasp through the pain. "I was thinking I'm in the hospital and don't know why."

Father drops into the chair beside my bed and rubs his face. "You don't remember?"

"No, and thinking hurts."

"You and Emma were idiots. You went out before a big storm, then you tried to ride home in it. The driver rolled into the ice cream parlor. You're lucky to be alive."

More blinking brings back memories that cause my eyes to clench shut again. It doesn't help. Visions of the world spinning and flipping make my hands shake. The sight of the chair coming through our window brings tears to my eyes.

"Emma?" I whisper.

"The bed beside you. She still hasn't woken up."

My gaze travels to the next bed. Bandages cover my sister's head, and her closed eyelids are black and blue. "Is she okay?"

"The doctors say she should be, but she's still out. It will take time. You seem to have healed faster, which they're telling me is a miracle. Again, what were you thinking?"

"I was thinking I didn't want to let Emma ride alone, and I didn't want to stay at the restaurant because I figured being out longer would only anger you more. Believe it or not, we don't like to be yelled at."

His brown eyes turn into a fierce scowl. "You're always putting yourself in danger. Why can't you listen to me? I only want your safety."

The desire to roll my eyes is strong, but the pounding in my head advises against it, so I push the nurse's button instead. "You want to control us. I went to see the doctor because I wasn't feeling well. Emma went with me for support. She insisted we get something to eat before heading home. The storm came in too fast."

"You know how quickly bad weather moves in, Naomi. That's no excuse. Use your head for once."

My own anger rises. "This wasn't my fault."

"It was Emma's?"

"It was neither. We made the best decision with what we had. If you weren't so uptight, maybe we wouldn't have pushed it to be home and wouldn't have taken the ride share to try to make it before you exploded at us for being out."

Dad's face turns red, and he opens his mouth for a barrage I'm sure will be unpleasant. He's interrupted by a nurse entering the room. She takes one look at the scene she walked into before putting her hands on her hips. "It's a good thing that she's awake, Mr. Morgan, but this is no time to upset her. If you can't behave, then you need to leave."

He opens his mouth and closes it. It's clear he doesn't trust himself to speak, so he grunts and gets up. His hand digs into his pocket, and he tosses a phone into my lap. "Your old one was destroyed in the accident. I have work to do."

As he stomps out of the room, the nurse shakes her head. It seems that I'm the only one that can break through his good father facade in public. I hold the power button until the phone logo shows on the screen. "Can I get something for my headache?"

"Of course. We expected this because you took quite a nasty knock to the head. You and your sister seemed to both have been knocked out by a chair."

She pulls a cart with a built-in computer into the room and over to my bed. She scans a paper packet that she opens, dropping two pills into my hand. After refilling my water pitcher, she pours me another cup of water. I take the medication, hoping for relief so badly that I don't even notice the unpleasant taste. They need better water filters in this building.

"How long have I been here?" I ask while she checks my monitors.

"About two days. You healed rather quickly. Too bad your sister doesn't have the same abilities."

I don't trust my father's answer. "Is she going to be alright?"

"It looks like she will be. It's just going to take some time for her to wake. She took a harder knock than you did, and like I said, she isn't healing as well as you."

"What about the driver?"

Her eyes turn sad. "He was gone when the emergency crew got to you. It looked to be instant."

"Oh," I whisper and look down at my hands. If we wouldn't have been looking for a ride, would he have been safe at home? Did we kill him? I should have convinced Emma that we should have waited. I gave up too easily. Despite my anger at Dad for blaming me, guilt flows through me.

The nurse pats me on the shoulder. "There's nothing you could've done. It happened quickly."

"We could have not hired him to drive us home."

She sighs. "You had no idea he'd crash. He also could have stayed home and not taken the money."

That's true, but it doesn't make me feel any better. With a gentle squeeze of my shoulder, she tells me to buzz if I need anything and walks out. At this point, my headache is losing some of its sharpness. I look over at Emma again.

She was out because of me. My sister was worried about me, which is not something I'm used to. I should have gone alone, but I have a feeling those arguments would have been as futile as the ones I made against riding home. She was only looking out for us. I should have done a better job at it as well.

As soon as my head clears enough, I unlock my new phone and put a passcode on it. Then I scroll through the apps and delete all the GPS programs Father put on it. I'm sure there are some I don't find, but I tried. Maybe when I'm feeling a little better, I can look harder. He doesn't check them often. It's still one of the reasons I don't like taking my phone when I go to the beach. I've simply been lucky he hasn't looked the few times that I did.

I start to download apps I want and log in to them. Social media is first, followed by games. The fitness app I never open comes next. Last, I decide to log into my email, feeling stupid because it may have made it easier to get everything else logged in. I'm probably still dealing with a little brain fog.

My phone ringing keeps me from looking further. "Hello?"

"Naomi, it's Lucy. I wanted to know how you were doing. Dad told us you're awake, but he looked angry when he said it."

Of course he did. Well, what else can I expect? It's not like Travis Morgan actually cares about his daughters' happiness. Is he mad about our talk, that I got hurt, or my attitude in general? If anything, I'd bet it's all of the above. There isn't much I do anymore that doesn't upset him. I don't feel bad about it either. I'm an adult and deserve my freedom. I've earned it.

I sigh into the phone. "I'm awake, but Emma is still unconscious."

"What happened? Dad only told us that you did something stupid."

Again, of course he did. "We tried to catch a ride back home in the storm. There was an accident. It seems we both got knocked on the head pretty hard. When I woke up, our father decided to dig into me and try to tear me a new one. I talked back, so I'm sure he's not happy about that."

"You have a talent for angering him, but he shouldn't be upsetting you when you just woke up after such a bad accident. That's not good."

"No, it's not. How is home?" Anything to change the subject.

"The usual. Fighting, noise, and lack of peace. You're not missing anything. I'd come visit, but Dad told us to leave you alone to think about what you've done."

I rub my eyes. "It's not like I tried to do this. I even tried to talk Emma out of riding home until the storm passed. I don't know why he makes everything my fault."

"He does seem to be overly harsh on you. Well, all of us, but mostly you."

Something she said occurs to me. "You wanted to visit?"

"I still do, but I don't have the courage to go against Dad like you do."

I almost laugh at how much good that's done for me, but I don't think it's the right moment to do so. Lucy is pretty sensitive to things, and I don't want her to think I'm laughing at her. The fact that she cares enough to want to visit is surprising. Why am I now only finding out I have two sisters that actually care? Or maybe they always have. Maybe I simply overlooked them with the hostility I deal with day-to-day.

That last option seems more likely. Living in that house has been pure misery. Mom sheltered me a bit from the bullying, but it was a free-for-all when she died. I was still grieving when it started too. With all that drama on top of my trauma, it's no wonder I just lumped them all together. I need to do better.

"How is school going?" I ask to start being a better sister to one of the ones that deserve it.

"Oh!" she says, sounding surprised I asked, which only makes me feel guiltier. "Good. I have some big tests coming up, but I think I'm ready."

We spend some time on easier topics before the screaming starts in the background. She apologizes and hangs up. It isn't much, but our conversation is a step in the right direction. I'm not as alone as I thought a few days ago. I need to open my eyes more. Not that I think any of the others are friendly. I know much better than that.

This time, I make it to my email. My eyes widen at the number of messages I have. They're all from the forum post I made right before the accident. I remember wanting to check for replies, but the accident got in the way. There are hundreds here, and I'm feeling overwhelmed to the point I don't even want to log into the forum to check them.

It might not be a good thing with the way I'm feeling. My head feels heavy, and my eyelids keep trying to shut. I'll give myself a nap before I decide to tackle the replies or not.

Chapter Fourteen
Stupid Actions

After a longer nap than expected, I find myself staring at my phone again. Do I want to check the replies? I think I've already decided mermaids are crazy talk. That doesn't mean someone not crazy wouldn't have contacted me with a real answer. Right?

Why are decisions so hard to make? Ones like these should be easy. Look or don't look. It's not like anyone could say anything that would shake my sanity. Could they?

I glance over at Emma again. As far as I know, she is still unconscious. The fact that I'm awake and she's not makes me worry. I don't care how much faster I am healing. She should still be awake by now if I'm feeling almost normal again.

I hope she does. I don't want to lose one of the good sisters I've come to have. Another loss can't happen. *Please wake up.*

Turning back to my phone, I tell myself I'm being a coward. Right before I can open the forum, another nurse enters. This time, I'm getting my blood taken, which makes me wonder about the last one I had done, so I ask about it.

"There were some anomalies but nothing overly worrisome. The last set we did yesterday looked normal. We're just going to check again."

"What kind of anomalies?"

"They're not sure. They couldn't isolate them enough to identify, and they're gone now. It could have simply been an issue with the lab."

I bite my lip to keep quiet and not sound paranoid. They weren't normal the first time either. The fact that it was twice in a row makes it hard to believe it was caused by contamination or error. I keep those thoughts to myself. I'm sure they know better than I about what is worrisome or not. Not something to worry about at the moment.

She draws a few vials of blood before doing the same for Emma. I watch her walk out and pick up my phone again. Before I can do anything, the door opens for yet another interruption that makes me want to sigh. My doctor walks in.

"Well, so far, everything is looking good. Keep this up, and we might let you go home soon," he says.

I offer a small smile for him, but I'm not sure if I want to go home. I'll need to deal with ridicule and anger. It might be crazy, but I'd rather stay in the hospital. Of course, I can't tell him any of that.

"Good," I say instead of what I really want to. "I'm ready to put this all behind me."

He opens my chart and looks at it. I let the smile fall. That last part wasn't a lie. Too bad I won't be able to put it all behind me when dealing with my father. If I mention that, it would only cause me more trouble. Father's reputation is too important to him to let me tarnish it. I can only imagine the punishments that will come if I do that.

"It looks like your PCP ordered an MRI?" the doctor says.

"Yeah, I was having some other issues."

"What kind of issues?"

Great. Like I want to tell more people I'm crazy. "Just some strange stomach issues and some hallucinations."

"Are you having any of that now?"

I think back over my time awake. Granted, I haven't been awake long. "No. Nothing like that."

"Well, since she ordered it and you missed the call because you were here, we'll have it done. Tell me more about these symptoms."

I sigh and repeat everything that's been happening to me since the day I found the scale, leaving out the parts that might get me committed. He doesn't need to know about the strangeness with Lenora or things I'm finding at the beach. I'll keep those ones to myself. Besides, I'm sure it's just my mind trying to drive me nuts by making connections where there are none.

By the time we're done talking, someone comes in with a wheelchair to take me to radiology. My doctor says, "Well, it seems as if it's not bothering you now, but it's best to have it looked at. I'll make sure the results get to your primary doctor as well."

The man transporting me helps me into the wheelchair. The elevator down makes my stomach lurch, but I figure it's just the medications I'm on and the sudden movement. A few floors down, he sits me by a door in an empty hall, and I find myself wishing I had my phone with me. They're taking forever to get me.

My mind goes through the accident again, and I try to shake the memories away. I don't want to remember the smile the driver had on his face when he realized who we were. I don't want to remember Emma's screams mixing with mine. The rain, the slide, the sound of glass shattering. Tears form in my eyes. I brush them away.

One man is dead. My sister is still unconscious. I don't need any more reminders of everything that happened and everything still wrong afterward. All I want is peace, which seems unachievable for me. Why can't everything just leave me alone?

By the time someone comes out to get me, my eyelids are dragging again, made worse by the burning from my traitorous tears. They wheel me in, helping me onto the table. Once I'm inside the machine, listening to all the noise it makes, I feel my eyes grow heavy again. I close them, sure I won't be able to fall asleep with this kind of racket.

The waves bob me up and down in the water. Eerie silence encompasses the world around me. Even the swells make no noise, adding a stronger sense of foreboding. Glancing around, I see the beach a decent swim behind me. Before trying to make it in, I move my hands to spin myself in a circle. Nothing else sticks out to my searching gaze.

Somehow, I find myself able to swim. This time, I'm not drowning. My arms slow their movements. Where did those thoughts come from? That makes no sense at all. I'm swimming now. Aren't I?

A splash pulls my thoughts out of their state of confusion. I turn my head to see a familiar shimmer just below the surface of the water a little further from the safety of the sand. My heart skips a beat before my arms start moving faster. Whether I can swim or not isn't important right now. I need to reach land.

When I glance back again, the shine is closer to me. The beach is too far away still, but that doesn't stop me from trying to hurry more. I may suddenly be able to swim, yet I can't do it fast enough.

Something brushes against my foot, and I scream into the weird silence. The sky grows dark as I fight to reach safety. Lightning flashes in the sky, making me sob. This time, scales run over the bottom of my kicking feet. I gasp.

A hand grabs my ankle and pulls me down. I can't see anything under the water, but the fear is almost enough to make me swallow the salty liquid. I kick out, toes grazing something hairy. The hand lets go.

When I break the surface again, I find the sandy land much closer. My feet find purchase, and I try to run through the rough water. Pain blossoms in my leg. I fall, swallowing a mouthful of saltwater. The pain in my leg increases. Screaming, I use my hands to pull myself out of the lapping tide while dealing with the tearing and pinching feelings in my calf.

I'm eventually out of the water, missing a leg like the boy on the beach. Crying, I try to climb further onto land, but the blood spouting out of me makes me sluggish. Another splash pulls my attention. Still, there is no sound beside me and whatever is after me.

A hand breaks above the water. Further back, a giant fishtail splashes again. I use my good leg and my hands to scramble backward. The head of a giant angler fish surfaces next, clicking sharp teeth at me. I scream, and a hand touches my shoulder.

Gasping, I sit up and find my leg is whole once more. I'm no longer on the beach. The MRI tech raises hands to calm me as I search for the creature that was trying to devour me. My breath comes in big gulps.

"It's okay. You fell asleep," the tech says. "Must have been one hell of a nightmare."

The world comes back to me, reminding me where I am. I push the horror away, which is something I'm getting better at. I'm not sure if that's a good thing or bad. "Yeah. It was scary. Did I ruin the MRI?"

"No. We got some great images. You didn't start to thrash until we were pulling you out of the machine. Are you okay?"

Nodding, I look around one last time to make sure all is normal. "I'd like to go back to my room now."

"Of course."

Within minutes, I'm back in the hall in my wheelchair, waiting for the transporter to return. I can't get the feeling of losing my leg out of my mind. Sometimes, I'll feel the pain piercing my flesh. My leg is whole when I look though. I just want the safety of my unconscious sister next to me.

After what seems like another eternity, I'm being pushed away. On the elevator, the lurch reminds me of the bobbing in the waves, panic rising again. I squeeze the arms of my chair and close my eyes. The man wheeling me through the halls gives me a look when he notices my tense state but says nothing. I guess traumatized people are normal in a hospital. I'm happy to climb back into my bed and pull my covers up to my chin.

Just a dream—a terrible and horrifying dream. That's all it was. Everything going on lately is culminating in my sleeping mind. My subconscious is torturing me. Is it guilt? I know I'm feeling a bit of that toward multiple people. Wouldn't it be showing me the crash if it was though?

I let my head fall back against the pillow again. This is hopeless. I can't think well enough to figure this out. It was a dream, so there probably isn't anything to figure out. I'm simply trying to assign meaning to my mind's rambling. My medications could also be messing with my dreams. I need rest, but I'm too scared to get it right now. What if the waves and the monster are waiting for me to close my eyes again?

One more look at Emma tells me I don't have anyone to talk it over with. Instead, I pick up my phone and decide to use the forums to distract me. The number of private messages astounds me. Most are insulting my intelligence for saying I don't believe in mermaids. Some are trying to convince me that they're real. Others are death threats, which seems like a horrible overreaction; particularly given my current environment.

Nothing helpful resides in my messages, so I move to my post to find more of the same. At least the death threats seem to stick to my private messages. I scroll past replies full of evidence and *truths*. I go through people asking me why I came to this forum if I'm just going to make fun of and invalidate them, which I don't feel like I was doing in the first place. I just want answers, and I didn't know where else to look for them.

It only makes me feel more alone. Do I and my beliefs belong anywhere? I'm ostracized at home. That attitude has followed me to the internet. I'm currently in the hospital with nobody to talk to besides keyboard warriors.

Coming to this site for a non-mermaid answer was obviously a grievous error on my part. Even people telling me why my scale and tooth are proof aren't helping because their reasons aren't concrete in my mind. I rub my eyes. Right when I'm about to delete my account and close the site forever, I find one response that is different from all the others.

That is a mermaid scale and tooth. I know this for a fact. I can tell by your post that you might not believe me, but please answer this question. Has anything strange happened since you found them? Anything at all? Strange sightings or feelings?

I chew on my lip and ignore all the comments telling the person who replied not to bother because I'm only here to make fun of them all. Many use my lack of response after so long to mean I'm a troll, as if there's no possibility I might have a good reason—a hospital stay, for example. I ignore it all, focusing only on his question. All that matters is the person who asks questions to make me think he might actually want to help instead of insulting and threatening me.

I can't bare my crazy to an online community that already seems to hate me, but what if he knows something? Not that I believe the first part of that reply, and I'll keep telling myself that as long as it takes to be convincing. That doesn't mean there might not be something here.

In the end, I can't help myself. *I apologize for the late reply. I've been in the hospital. What kind of strange things?*

Closing the website, I toss my phone onto the rolling tray beside my desk. I bury my face in my hands and take a few deep breaths. I truly am an idiot.

Chapter Fifteen
Hard Noodles

The TV echoes as channels are flipped from one to the next. I look over at Emma, who is sitting bright and alert. She woke up earlier today and has only napped twice. I take that as a good sign.

We've talked and worked through our shared trauma a bit, but we've been otherwise keeping it light. One go over of the accident is more than enough. I know that we will both need to examine everything further in the near future to fully process it. Now, we just want to heal without dwelling more than necessary. Although, if she's like me, she's doing plenty of dwelling in silence.

I shake my dark thoughts away, unwilling to let them destroy the joy of both of us awake and healing. "How are you feeling?" I ask for the hundredth time.

"Alive, but groggy. Same as the last twenty times you've asked."

Has it only been twenty? "They're letting me go home tomorrow morning, so you'll get a break from the question."

She chuckles softly. "Well, some alone time wouldn't hurt. I'm surprised Dad hasn't dropped by since I woke up. Maybe he's busy."

"He usually is, but I also pissed him off earlier."

Emma turns her gaze to me. Her blonde hair is shaved on one side, a line of stitches showing through what used to be thick locks. I wince and look away. My head wound was on my forehead, so I didn't take any extra grooming. My sister definitely got it worse than me.

"What is he mad at now?" she asks.

"My stupidity."

When I look back, her brown eyes show confusion. "But I'm the one that insisted on hiring someone to drive us home in the storm. You told me you thought we should wait it out. How is that your fault?"

"Well, you were out in it because of me in the first place."

Emma scoffs. "That doesn't make it your fault. What is his reasoning?"

"I'm going to guess that the reasoning is that it's always my fault."

She sighs and leans back against her pillow again. I can tell this conversation is wearing her out, which sends another pang of guilt shooting through me. She needs her rest to recover faster. I should let her get what she needs.

"He does seem to be really hard on you, more than any of the rest of us," she says after a bit. Her voice sounds tired. "I wonder why that is."

"Maybe because I'm the one that's more openly defiant of his rule over us."

"Could be."

My sister's eyes start to drift shut, but they open again when the door latch clicks. A woman holding a tray walks in. She sets it on my table and rolls it over me. I thank her and receive a nod of acknowledgement. I lift the cover to find pasta shells and meatballs covered in tomato sauce.

"That smells heavenly," Emma says.

"Sorry," I say.

"I'll get there eventually. No need to feel bad on my account."

I stab a few shells with my fork and bring them to my mouth. This is the first real food they've let me have since I woke up, and I'm going to savor it. When I bite down, the pasta sticks to my teeth, way under cooked. I use my nails to pry the food loose and spit it out.

"By the look on your face," Emma says, "I think I'll hold on to my IV nutrition for as long as possible. Liquid nutrients don't turn my stomach."

"Good idea," I mutter.

Instead of going back to the pasta, I try the burnt garlic toast that sits on the edge of my tray. A little bland, but at least it's cooked, if a little too much so. Cautious, I stick a meatball in my mouth next. Those actually aren't bad.

"Maybe I should ask for just meatballs next time," I say.

When Emma doesn't answer, I look over to see her asleep again. I lift the remote she put on the table beside us and turn off the TV to keep it from disturbing her. I finish off the edible parts of my meal, then eat an unripe banana and drink my little carton of grape juice, glad my strange tastes didn't follow me to the hospital.

The nurse walks in to check vitals, noticing my uneaten pasta. "Appetite feel off?"

I shake my head. "The pasta just wasn't to my taste. The meatballs were good though."

"Well, you got some food into you. The doctor will be by in a few minutes to discuss your test results."

Emma sleeps through the checking of vitals, and the nurse walks out. I fidget with the edge of my blanket, wondering what my MRI shows. There has to be some cause of these nightmares and hallucinations if my blood work keeps coming back fine. The other option is that I'm simply crazy. That's something I don't want to even contemplate.

The doctor walks in with my chart in hand. "Good evening, Ms. Morgan. Going home tomorrow."

"Look forward to it." Only half a lie after that meal.

"So, your blood work is perfect. Your MRI doesn't show anything concerning. Everything looks normal, so I'm confident that sending you home is still the best course."

"Nothing to explain all the strangeness I've been noticing?"

He shakes his head. "Nothing at all. Your health is squeaky clean. Have you been overly stressed lately?"

I want to laugh. When am I not stressed? Then again, lately it does seem to be worse. I think my need for freedom is pushing me against the grain to the point I'm making things escalate. Not that I'll tell him that. I'm not that much against the grain yet.

My doctor must read some of my thoughts through the expressions on my face, if not the reason behind them. "It's possible that your mind is trying to cope with different stressors. Why don't I give you the card of our resident therapist?"

"You want me to see a shrink?"

"I want you to talk to someone to find out what might be behind your symptoms. The mind is a powerful and mysterious thing, Ms. Morgan. Stress can do a lot to your brain. Take a chance to talk to someone about what's been bothering you. It may help you sleep easier."

He takes a card out of his pocket to hand to me. Reluctant, I take it between my fingers as if it might burn me. He offers me a reassuring smile and tells me he'll see me tomorrow morning before I'm released. After he's gone, I flip the card around in my fingers without really looking at it.

Dad would love this. His youngest daughter talking to someone about her crazies. If the newspapers get hold of that information, I'll never hear the end of it. If he even finds out I'm going, I'll wish I never touched this card.

The biggest thing holding me back from accepting this is that I don't think I need it. Yes, I'm stressed. No, talking to some stranger about it isn't going to help. And what am I going to tell this therapist? I have a mermaid scale and tooth hidden at home, and they're causing all kinds of strange occurrences? That'll go over well. Straight jacket, here I come.

"No, thank you," I mutter.

With a glance at my sleeping sister, I lean over to toss the business card in the trash and grab the remote. I turn the TV back on but keep the volume low. Channel after channel goes by. I think I agree with Emma; TV sucks.

A video of my father makes my finger pause over the channel up button. He's talking about some new policy meant to keep our beaches cleaner. I scoff, knowing that it's only an attempt to keep voters interested. He doesn't care about the beach because he's too afraid of it. He thinks it's dangerous to the point he doesn't let his daughters visit it. I shake my head and turn the channel again.

Channel surfing ends on a wildlife documentary. I watch lions chase zebras for a bit before picking up my phone. Again, I have a bunch of emails notifying me of replies to my post. I open the forums.

More hate meets my eyes. Skimming over it, I search for one in particular. When I find it, I ignore all the angry replies to my reply, scrolling until I see that the user who answered me without hoping I'd die did reply.

From my experience, that would be nightmares, both waking and sleeping. Maybe seeing strange things and having strange feelings.

Nightmares, both waking and asleep? Is that what the hallucinations are? Are my bad dreams seeping into my time awake? They started first. I think.

Ugh. Rubbing my eyes, I hold back a groan. This is impossible. Everything seems to be blurring together. You would think this has all been long term and not just the short time it has been. I don't even remember when it all started, only the thing that I feel triggers it.

And that's a thought that makes me feel insane.

I push it into the back of my mind, trying to decide if I want to answer this person or go ahead with my earlier plans of deleting my account and pretending I never posted. The latter seems to be the smartest course. As we've learned, I'm not known for taking the smartest course. Can't disappoint.

Maybe. I mean, I never described anything like that, but it could fit. I don't really want to talk about it in this hostile environment.

My fingers hover over the letters on my screen for a few seconds. What else can I say without giving away too much? I'll only be attacked more by the idiots who can't handle someone thinking a different way than them. I don't believe what they do, so I deserve death threats and hateful messages.

Sighing, I simply hit send. I feel like they have to drag information out of me, but I don't want to really say much more than that where everyone else can see it. It's bad enough thinking I'm crazy. I don't want others confirming. Maybe I shouldn't have answered. The second option of pretending the forums never happened looks better by the second.

For some reason, I don't. Instead, I go back to watching a lioness take down a full-grown striped horse. Watching the feline tear into her prey makes me shudder. My mind strays back to my most recent beach visits, so I push those thoughts away and turn the TV off.

Emma still emits soft snores. My eyes burn to the point I feel the need to close them, but I don't. Instead, I stare at the dark ceiling and listen to Emma sleeping in the bed next to me. The monitors let off a soft glow that doesn't touch most of the surface above me. I focus on those dark spots and wonder once again how my life turned into this.

I've always hated my lot in life. I lost my mother while still young. Most of my sisters can't stand to be around me without something nasty to say. Dad won't let me have a life. It's been a long and bleak existence.

Somehow, my life found a way to take a turn for the worse. At this point, I'd give anything to go back to the bleakness I've lamented for so long. At least things made sense then, even if I didn't like the sense they made. No hallucinations. I still had my precious box. No creepy woman or internet full of people trying to convince me that mermaids exist. No deaths that make me feel immense guilt.

How do I backtrack to something I told the universe over and over that I didn't want? I don't want this uncertainty and insanity. I don't want me and my sister to be healing in hospital beds. I don't want to question the stability of my mind.

Why me? Why does life want to keep beating me down? I can't handle the uncertainty and mystery. All I want is to live my life. Right now, I'm even willing to give up the stipulation to live it like I want to. What do I do?

Chapter Sixteen
Had Enough

I'm woken by someone entering our room. Emma is already up, leafing through some magazine one of the nurses must have brought. My doctor follows the morning nurse in with a smile.

"Time to go home, Ms. Morgan." He looks between us. "Er, Ms. Naomi Morgan."

Emma laughs. "I already assumed it wasn't me."

"I figured I needed to make that clear," he says with an even brighter smile. "Okay, Naomi. I'm happy with everything I'm seeing. I'll have one of the nurses call your father for a ride. Take some time to eat breakfast before you leave. Once your ride is here, get on out of here."

"Okay. I won't mind getting out of this bed."

As much as I don't want to deal with my family at home, I do mean that last point. I'm starting to miss the feeling of the sun on my face. Despite how my latest beach trips turned out, I also miss the sound of the ocean. I'll need to make a visit sometime soon.

The doctor checks over Emma's latest tests and tells her he wants her to try to eat something light. As soon as he turns away from her, my sister grimaces, which makes it hard to hold back my laughter. No more liquid nutrition for her.

As soon as he's out the door, I say, "I don't suggest anything with noodles."

Emma makes a face that causes me to giggle. I check the menu and decide that pancakes might be a safe bet. She sticks with toast and jello.

We keep the conversation light while we wait. Once the food comes, we focus on that.

The pancakes are pretty good. I'd like a little more butter and syrup, but even dry pancakes are better than the pasta I had last night. It comes with burnt sausage, which I eat as well, the charred flavor not turning me off enough to make me stop. While meat still seems to taste best to me, I'm not turning my nose up at other food.

Maybe some time in the hospital for a reset fixed whatever issues I had. I don't need any therapist. I have this. A few days of not needing to worry about anything are making me feel much better. I'm not crazy, mermaids aren't real, and the world is as it should be. I just needed some time away from the hectic world that is the Morgan household.

Arabella steps into the room. "Are you ready?"

Her tone makes me want to flinch. She's impatient while I dress in the clothes she brought, barely spending any time acknowledging that Emma is awake. Father will probably come visit my sister now that I'm out. I'm not sure if she'll be lectured as well or not, but he will make sure she's alive and being treated as befits the daughter of the mayor.

Arabella leaves to bring the car to the front of the hospital. I climb into my mandatory wheelchair and say goodbye to Emma with hopes she'll be back soon. The drive home is uncomfortable. My driver squeezes the steering wheel hard enough that her knuckles turn white. I try to ignore her ire and watch the town go by outside the window.

As we pull into the driveway, she turns to me. "When will you learn to get in line?"

Blinking, I can only stare for a moment. "What?"

"Stop stressing Father out. He has a whole town to take care of. Your defiance stresses him out more. You're so ungrateful."

My body stiffens. "Ungrateful for what? Being trapped in a life under someone else's control? I didn't ask to be put in the hospital."

"But you didn't act in a way that would keep you out of it either. Father only wants our safety. He wants what's best for us. I don't understand how you can't see that. He has given up everything to give us good lives."

Incredulous, I laugh. "Good lives? Arabella, he sees us as nothing but property he needs to control. That's not living. Most of us can't drive or get jobs because we aren't kissing his ass hard enough that he trusts us to fall in line. Also, tell me what exactly he's given up."

Her lips press tightly for a moment. "Seriously, Naomi? Do you always need to be so callous and vulgar? With your attitude, you wonder why he doesn't trust you more. You don't want to fall into line, but that line is the best place to be."

Rolling my eyes, I open the door, step out, and slam it shut. Arabella's mouth moves, but I can't hear her anymore. Not that it matters. I can guarantee it's not something complimentary. She backs back out of the driveway and heads toward town. I let out a strong gust of air through my nostrils.

Not even in the door, and I need to deal with her lectures. Good thing Dad will be at work now; I don't need more self-righteous anger directed at me. It used to be my motto to try to fall under their radar. Be quiet. Don't argue. Deescalate.

That's not happening anymore. I'm sick and tired of being treated like I don't deserve better. I'm tired of being lectured and attacked. Time to fight back. A group of my sisters is spread across the entryway and living room. Doing my best to ignore them, I make my way to the stairs.

Brooke accosts me before I can reach them. "The freak's back. Seems like the lesser sister came home first."

I turn on her, the fury from everything happening hitting me all at once. "Sorry if I can't find it in myself to allow my mind to be fogged by drugs to keep living dulled to this hell. Why don't you go back to your pack of meth heads and leave me alone? I'm actually trying to do something with my life that doesn't involve watching it go by through a fog."

Brooke's mouth drops open in shock. A glance around me shows that everyone else wears the same expression. I send a glare around to all of them, softening it when I see Lucy staring at me with wide eyes through the dining room doorway. Before anyone can recover enough to retaliate, I turn and stomp quickly up the steps.

I slam my door, leaning against it with my eyes closed and taking deep breaths. I can't believe I did that. All my life, I've done my best to avoid conflict. Leave it to my family to bring it out of me. I may have shocked all of them, but no one is as surprised as I am right now. That felt so good.

A knock shakes the wood at my back. I flinch and wonder if I have the stamina to stand up for myself with the retaliation I know is coming. Taking a few deep breaths, I straighten and yank open the door.

The scowl leaves my face. "Hey, Lucy."

She gives me a shy smile. "Can I come in?"

Nodding, I back up a few steps to let her in. Before closing the door, I stick my head out to look down the hall. No waiting ambush. That's good. Maybe they're all still stunned.

When I close the door, Lucy holds out a box. "This came for you yesterday. I happened to see it on the porch before anyone else and kept them from opening it."

"Thank you," I say, taking the mysterious package. "About what happened downstairs..."

Lucy waves her hands at me. "Don't worry about it. Brooke deserved it and more. I wish I had the courage to stand up for myself like that."

"I usually value peace over conflict, but I'm tired and didn't need that the second I walked through the front door after everything."

"I understand. How do you feel?"

"A lot better."

Lucy gives me a warm smile that looks less shy. "Good. Are you going to open it, or do you want me to leave?"

"What?" She glances at my hands, reminding me of the package. "Oh, right. I don't mind your company."

We sit on the bed, and I open the box with a pair of scissors. Inside another beach treasure covered container holds my gaze. Why in the world did she send me another one? She can't know I threw the last one away. Can she?

"That's pretty," Lucy says, startling me enough that I jerk. Her gaze turns sheepish. "Sorry. Didn't know I'd scare you by speaking up."

"It's alright."

"The box is really beautiful, but you don't look happy."

I take a deep breath, putting the cursed object on my bed and rubbing my eyes. "It is beautiful. I'm just feeling off and tired."

"I'll go then. Get some rest. After everything you've been through, I'm sure you need it."

As soon as she closes the door behind her, I flip the top of the box open to find another folded piece of paper. For a brief moment, I consider throwing it all away without looking at the note. My curiosity grows too strong.

I know you lost the second box I gave you. Please, be more careful with this one. They take a lot of work to make.

~L

I grit my teeth hard enough to feel pain. There's no way she knows. Maybe Lenora saw something in my face the night of the banquet. One thing's for sure, I'm not keeping this thing. The more that woman interacts with me, the more she creeps me out. As if I don't have enough other things going on that do that. I don't need her adding to it.

Angry at her insistence, I open the door and stick my head out again. All clear. I quietly walk down the stairs, happy to find the bottom floor empty now. I hurry out to the garbage can and drop the jewelry box in it. Let's hope I don't end up needing to deal with another surprise *gift*.

I stop by the kitchen to make a roast beef sandwich with cheddar and mayo. Back in my room, I sit down to eat and stare out the window. The sky is bright blue with few clouds. Those that do float in the blue expanse are white and fluffy, not the ominous darkness of the last ones I saw. I swallow past the lump that the memories put in my throat and look away.

Emma's still in the hospital. I'm out in the bright sunshine while living in darkness. If anyone deserves to be home, it's Emma. My sister creates art to bring joy. I simply wallow in self-pity over my lack of freedom. She tries to use her art to make others happy. She should be the one tasting freedom right now. Rubbing my eyes, I finish off the sandwich that now tastes like ash.

"I need to actually do something with my life. I'm pathetic," I mutter into the silence.

Instead of changing my life, I only complain about it. I need to stop spending money on inconsequential items. Immediate needs only. This town holds me prisoner under my father's thumb. If I can find my way to a new town, I can maybe start over.

I bite my lip. "It's not like I have many skills."

Shaking my head, I push the words down. Many people in life do just fine without skills. If I can just find some steadiness, I can try to get some education like Lucy. Up until now, that thought hasn't really come to me because I know Dad doesn't trust me enough to pay for schooling. That's fine. When I'm on my own, I'll find a way to pay for it myself.

Well, now I know what I want to do. How do I go about it? Father will know if I'm not using my allowance. I need to withdraw it and stash it away somehow. Gift Cards might work. The withdrawals will show as just another transaction at a store. That seems to be the best way I can get away. I'm not quite sure how to convert those back to cash, but I'll think about it later.

None of this matters at the moment. My allowance account is low right now, so I can't start hoarding yet. I should be getting another deposit in a week's time. I just need to hold out until then. I can live poorly. This shouldn't be that hard. Maybe I can talk Lucy and Emma into coming with me. Roommates will make things less expensive for each of us.

I know Emma is nervous about the idea, but I don't think she was totally against it when I mentioned it before. Once we're out of here, he can't touch us. We're adults. We'll leave a note, so he can't say we were kidnapped. Lucy may not have the courage to leave. Even if she does, Dad is paying for her education. She'll want to finish that first. That's fine. She can come whenever she wants.

Satisfied, I lift my phone and unlock the screen. I left it on the forum site and decide to put all this behind me too. Before I can close it, a notification saying I have a message shows up. I press the button without thought, finding a message from the person I've been talking to.

We need to talk.

Chapter Seventeen
Defiance

Pacing for the last hour has done nothing to tell me what I should do. I tried to ask the person what we need to talk about, but the only answer I got was that it's best to talk, not text. Should I contact this person? Should I let this all back in the dust of my escape plans?

"What do I do?" I growl, bouncing a bit in frustration.

I look at my phone to see they've said something else. *I'm serious. It's important that I talk to you.*

Another growl escapes, and I make another circle around my room before answering. *I don't even know who you are. The death threats I've gotten over my post are unbelievable. How do I know you're not one of them trying to trick me into letting my guard down?*

Because I'm not. Listen... My name is Stephen Moore from North Dakota. You can put my name and information anywhere for me to be found by someone if you go missing. Will you trust me then? Your life is at stake.

That seems a little dramatic. Still, my heart hiccups a moment when I reread his words. All my nightmares return to the front of my mind, along with the teen's missing leg, the dolphin pod, and the dead dog. All of that happened in the ocean. I'm on land.

I take a deep breath and begin typing. *Well, Stephen Moore from North Dakota, I don't see how my life is in danger. I have a lot of real things to worry about. Mermaids can't even enter my mind.*

I pace back and forth a little longer before the reply comes. *I bet you dream of drowning when you aren't in the water. You have moments of distress that are only calmed by water. You're seeing things about yourself that you can't believe are possible. You crave meat, particularly seafood. Is something dangerous following you in the waves?*

Gasping, I toss my phone onto my bed. They're guesses. They have to be. There's no way he can understand what's going on with me. I take a shaky breath and look back out at the sunlight that seems too bright to be real. Maybe this is some kind of disease, and he knows someone else that went through it. Since it's unknown, it looks like something out of fiction. That would make the most sense.

Trying to think of an answer, I look back at my phone to see that he sent another message. *I'm right, aren't I? That's why you haven't answered yet.*

Annoyance over him thinking he knows me takes over. *One, it hasn't been that long since you typed the last message. Maybe I'm looking at my phone thinking you're crazy. Two, you know nothing about me.*

Answer the question.

Tired of being pushed around, I throw my phone back on my bed. This is freaking ridiculous. This man is insane. He doesn't get to tell me what to do. My fingers twitch to answer, but I hold back. He needs to know that he's not in charge here. I'm tired of being walked all over.

After I feel a sufficient time to get my point across has passed, I pick my phone up again. *I don't know who you think you are, but you can't just say jump and expect me to jump. Those were just lucky guesses.*

Let's start easy. I apologize for telling you what to do. Can you tell me your first name? I don't need a last or a location like I gave you. I simply want to have something to call you besides forum poster.

A brief contemplation later, I realize he can't do much with my first name. *Naomi.*

Okay, Naomi. I've seen what's happening to you before. Someone close to me went through it. Please, video chat with me.

Like hell that's going to happen. I barely know this guy. What if he's some kind of pervert? Although, I'd be lying if I said I wasn't intrigued. Isn't this why I made that stupid post to begin with?

Sighing, I type, *I'm not comfortable with video, but voice would be okay*, then my phone number. My thumb hovers over the send button while I wonder how many more stupid things I'm going to do. I want answers, so I press it.

My phone rings in less than a minute. Swallowing hard, I answer, "Hello?"

"Naomi?"

"Stephen?"

I hear him sigh. "I'd rather do video, but if this is the only way you're comfortable, fine. We seriously need to talk."

"About mermaids?"

"I know it's hard to believe when the entire world tells you they're nothing but fairytales, but they are so much more than you think. You don't have to believe me right now. Please, just listen."

Taking a deep breath, I decide I've come this far. "Alright."

Murmurs come through the call, and Stephen asks me to hold on. He must put his hand over the phone because silence meets me before I can answer. His hand must slip. "Why the hell would you do that? We aren't in high school anymore, Brad."

More murmurs, followed by, "Shit, okay."

Stephen must drop his phone because I need to pull mine from my ear at the loud bangs to keep my hearing intact. His voice comes back. "Sorry, Naomi. I hope I didn't hurt your ear too much."

"You didn't."

"Okay, here's the thing. My roommate is an immature idiot." A defensive *hey* comes through the background noise. "He did something really stupid and needs a ride to the hospital, like now. Can I call you tomorrow afternoon?"

"Uhh, sure."

"Good. I'm going to get this knucklehead sorted out and have work in the morning, but I'll call you as soon as I get off."

"Okay."

"Is that your new girlfriend?" comes through the phone.

Stephen sighs. "Ignore him. He peaked in junior high. Promise me one thing."

"What's the promise?"

"Stay away from the ocean. Don't let the saltwater even touch you. This is extremely important."

What? Why would this be important? I've just decided not to let my father rule my life anymore and not to let my sisters concern me. This means more beach trips. Why should I avoid that?

"Naomi, please. At least until you hear from me again. Stay out of the water."

I sigh. "Fine."

We hang up, and I look at the screen. I never go into the water anyway. That really isn't a hard promise to keep. I'm still going to the beach tomorrow morning. No one can stop me. I'm tired of being told I can't do what brings me peace. I need to make a stand. Stephen won't stop me from doing that because I won't let him. If I'm going to defy my father, a stranger doesn't stand a chance. Sand isn't water though, so I'm not breaking the promise with my morning routine.

A knock echoes in my room. I jump. "What?"

"Time for supper," Clara says with even more haughtiness than normal.

"I'm not hungry."

"You've missed quite a few. Daddy won't be happy."

I scoff. "When is he happy with me?"

"Whatever. I don't mind giving him the news. You seem to love punishment."

Her footsteps fade down the hall. I take a few deep breaths, calming myself further. For some reason, my adrenaline feels high. There's no way I'm leaving my room right now though. I'll just need to pace some more to wear off the energy.

I must pace for longer than I realize because I hear another knock at my door. No one would come to bother me until supper is done, so time must have passed quickly. Opening the door, I fight the urge to slam it in the face on the other side.

"We need to talk, Naomi," my father says with a scowl.

I grit my teeth and consider slamming the door anyway. As if he can sense my hesitation, he lightly pushes me aside and closes it behind him. Walking over to my window, I cross my arms over my chest and stare at him with little warmth.

"Don't you dare look at me like that. This is still *my* house," he says.

"One I'm not allowed to leave."

"You haven't proven that you're trustworthy enough to handle that decision."

I almost laugh, holding the dark chuckle in at the last second and almost choking on it. "I'm an adult, Mayor. I can make my own decisions without your input."

"To you, I'm your father, and you will treat me as such. This defiance needs to stop, or I'll cut your allowance until you recognize who is out here working their ass off for you."

"You work only for yourself and keep us imprisoned to keep us from embarrassing you."

Dad rubs his face with his palms, giving his eyes extra attention with the heels of his hands. "I only want what's best for you. You have no idea what kind of evil hides outside these walls."

I roll my eyes. "I'm not naïve, Dad. I know the world isn't a bright place, not everything is good. You need to trust that I can handle myself."

"Not all things are easily handled."

Growling, I turn to look out over the darkening sky. Small pinpricks of light tell me the stars are getting ready to come out. How can I learn to handle things if he doesn't let me try? Somehow, I feel that this point will go right over his head. Mayor Morgan is not one to give up what he wants and admit he's wrong. I tuck my hair behind my ear and look down. It's hopeless.

If he takes away my allowance, I won't be able to save in an effort to run away. A nineteen-year-old trying to run away from home. It's sad I have to look at it that way. Why can't he treat me well enough to make me want to stay? Instead, he pushes me away by trying to control me.

When I refuse to argue, he grunts. "Very well. You leave me little choice. If you continue to defy my rules, I will pull your allowance out from under you. You will get no other warnings. Not only are you supposed to follow those rules, but I expect you at dinner from now on. We are a family. It's about time you acted like it."

I don't turn to look at him as I hear him stand and open the door. He pauses for a second. "This really is for your own good."

Dad slams the door behind him, and I finally turn. Tears sting my eyes as I stare at the wood blocking my escape. This isn't fair. I can't give up my freedom, but I also can't lose the only source of income I have. What do I do?

Freedom is more important than money, but money will give me a chance at greater freedom. I squeeze my eyes shut and take a few deep breaths. When I go to bite my lip, I taste blood. Startled, my hand flies to my mouth, feeling sharp points at the end of my teeth.

"No! Please, not now. I can't take this anymore."

I rush to the bathroom. Before I can cross the threshold and place my feet on the cool tiles, the ability to breathe leaves me again. Terrified that this keeps happening, I try to call for help. Not a sound escapes my mouth. I'd sob if I could, but I settle for letting tears stream down my cheeks.

Stumbling, I make my way toward the tub. The mirror won't help because my vision is turning foggy. It's not that I don't know what they look like. This isn't the first time I've seen them. Vicious thirst takes over as I turn the water on.

Without removing my clothes, I step into the tub and plug the drain before shoving my face under the faucet and drinking in hopes of finding relief. To my horror, my nails harden into what look like purple and blue scales, sharp enough to cut. As soon as the water is high enough, I sink below the surface.

Like before, the suffocation stops. This time, I am plagued by intense hunger as well. I fight down the urge to go looking for something to sink my teeth into. After a few minutes, it all recedes, and I feel like I'm drowning. Gasping, I pull myself out of the tub and lay on the floor like a heap of wet clothes. Maybe the doctor is right; it didn't happen again until I was home and stressed out. I'm finally able to sob and climb from the tub as the world goes black.

Chapter Eighteen
Caught

I wake shivering and covered in goosebumps. Sleeping in wet clothes on a hard floor isn't advised. I'm starting to wonder if I should put an air mattress in the bathroom since I seem to pass out here so much. My dark humor leaves me as quickly as it comes.

Groaning, I push myself into a sitting position, then strip my wet clothes off. Once on my feet with my pants off, I look in the mirror to see that everything is normal. Not that I didn't expect it when every other time has had no after effect. I pull the drain plug from the freezing tubful of water, then walk into my bedroom to look for something warm to put on.

It's still dark out, so I look at my phone. Dawn is only an hour away. I take a deep breath with the wave of longing that washes over me. My morning routine has been so thoroughly interrupted that my heart hurts. If I go to the beach, Father will cut my alliance to further trap me. Does he suspect my plan to make a run for it?

This isn't fair. He's denying me the one thing that brings peace and calm while I'm going through the worst turmoil I've ever faced. It's not like I can tell him what's going on, so I understand why he doesn't know. The only answers I'm receiving are ones that I don't believe. What would I even tell him? Would he care at all?

I need something good in my life, particularly now. Screw this. I'm going. If he cuts my allowance, I'll simply find another way. I'm not giving up on my plans, but I will find new ways to accomplish them if needed. Freedom won't mean anything if I've already lost hope and sanity. Besides, I have a strange urge to return to the sand.

Decided, I stand and slip my sandals on before heading to the door. Most people are still sleeping when I walk out of my room, but a few are awake. Father is in the master bathroom as I pass his room. It doesn't matter. I don't care what he threatens because I need this.

Clara sneers as I pass her in the hall, but I don't pay her any mind. Instead, I hurry down the stairs and out into the darkness that's being overtaken by a soft glow in the east. I head toward the brightening sky, not bothering to circumvent the center of town this time. As soon as my feet sink into the sand, I breathe a sigh of relief.

I've missed this. The salty scent of the ocean. The crashing of the waves. The feeling of the damp breeze coming off the water as the sun slowly turns the world from dark to light. The fright given to me by whatever lives in the sea doesn't matter. This is what I am meant for.

Glancing around to make sure no one can hear, I smile and bring my voice to life. The song my mother taught me bursts from my throat, happy to be released after so long trapped deep within. Careful to avoid the water on my toes, I walk along the line where the dry sand turns wet. I promised not to get wet, so I won't.

My voice continues to carry while I ignore the sounds of splashes in the water. There's nothing out there. No mermaid. No deadly predator. No stalker. All that's here is me and salty air. Bending down, I fish out something shining in the sand.

A shell that's an odd shade of purple comes up in my hand. The corner is chipped and cracked. I take the treasure a little further from the water and sit in the sand while rubbing my thumb over the smooth surface. My voice continues to flow.

"A nice voice you have there."

Startled, I drop the shell from my fingers and look up at the surprise voice beside me. A man that looks about my age stands above me with a cocky grin. Blinking, I look around to see the sun is just above the horizon and other beach goers are arriving. The mystery man clears his throat, the grin replaced by a scowl.

"Sorry. Thank you for the compliment. I didn't realize people were coming onto the beach," I say.

Standing, I ready myself to continue walking. If I want any treasures, I should get to them before others do. As I turn to leave, the guy grabs my wrist.

"Where are you off to in such a hurry?" he asks.

I turn and gaze at his fingers firmly clutching my arm, a frown forming on my face. "I have things I would like to do before it gets too crowded. If you would please let go, I'd like to get back to it."

"Whatever you were doing isn't that important, I'm sure. Not if you sat down and sang until you lost track of time. You have a really beautiful voice, and I'd like to see what else it could do."

My blood turns cold. "Excuse me?"

"Let's find somewhere we can enjoy each other's company."

"No thank you." I try to pull my hand free, but he only grips harder. The bones in my wrist shift under the pressure of his grip.

"Don't be like that. It's obvious that I like what I see. Don't you feel the same?"

"No, I don't. What I see is a man who can't take no for an answer."

I kick him in the ankle. His grip loosens enough for me to pull free. I run toward the group of people approaching from the boardwalk. When I look back, I see the guy glaring at me, but he isn't in pursuit. I slow.

I'm tired of pushy men telling me what I have to do. Glancing around, I see a family setting up on the dry part of the beach about halfway between the boardwalk and the water. I settle in close to them.

My treasure hunt may be ruined, but I'm not leaving. My father can't keep me from the peace of the ocean. Neither can the asshole smirking at me as he joins another group further from the one I'm using as a safety net. I may not be hunting for things to add to my box, but that doesn't mean I can't still enjoy my small touch of freedom.

Instead of filling my time scouring the sand, I watch the couple build a sandcastle with their children. I smile. They must have gotten up early to get here at this time. I wonder if it was the adult's decision or the kids' impatience. What would it have been like to have my family here when we were younger?

Arabella would probably have been bored. Clara would have been complaining about the sand going everywhere. Brooke's activity of choice is bullying, so it's probably good she's not here. The beach is more peaceful without Abigail's constant anger. Emma would like it here. I bet she'd make the best sandcastles. Lucy would probably have her face in a book. Our father would be on his laptop or phone.

Maybe not coming as a family is a good thing, even when we were children. All that sounds rather chaotic. A yell pulls me out of my thoughts, and I look toward the source.

The young man that accosted me not long ago looks slightly alarmed, chest deep in the water with his buddies. "Something just bit me."

"It was probably just a crab."

"A crab doesn't feel like that, dick. It really hur—"

The guy yelps and jumps. Alarm is replaced by terror as he tries to make his way to the beach. Now, his friends are not laughing. When I see the dark spot spreading in the water around the pushy asshole, my eyes widen. I jump to my feet.

"Is that blood?" someone further down the beach says.

As soon as the words hit my ears, the guy is yanked back. He stumbles and falls with a scream. I move closer but am careful not to touch the water, ever watchful of the promise I made to the stranger who believes in mermaids. The man disappears under the water. The dark circle widens further and faster.

His buddies yell and run for the beach, leaving him to fend for himself. He surfaces, long gashes cut deep into his face. The skin of his cheek hangs loose, and I feel the bile rise as the strips sway with his movements.

Once again, he tries to make it back to dry land. A few people move in to watch what happens from a closer vantage, unwilling to put themselves in danger but not fearing enough to avoid going in knee deep. Someone in a boat drives over to the struggling man. When he comes back up, they grab his frantically reaching hand.

Only to be pulled in when he goes under again. The rescuer scrambles to climb back in before becoming a second course. This time, when the man surfaces, he's not moving. Sirens wail in the near distance, but my eyes remain on the scene in front of me. The person in the boat pulls the man in and heads to shore. Others finally feel safe enough to help and drag the boat over the sand.

They drag the young man out, and I gasp and turn away. Where his stomach was, there is nothing but a large, gory hole. Worse, he's still alive. He may have scared me and had nefarious plans, but no one deserves this.

As the police and paramedics hurry in, I hear someone behind me say that he's gone. I can't look back. Instead, my eyes scan the crowd gathering around the scene. They fall on my father's, and I suppress a wince as he stomps over.

"Naomi Morgan," he says with a quiet growl that won't reach his supporters. "I told you that this was your last chance. Your allowance is gone. Get home. We will discuss this later."

By discuss, he means he will yell at me. Before I can answer, he's pushing past the onlookers to speak with the police. I swallow hard, taking a step to follow his orders, but I stop mid-step. I'm already in trouble, so what's a little more? I need to see.

Turning, I gasp and cover my mouth. Not only is his entire abdomen chewed away, but bite marks and long gashes cover his entire body, some body parts barely hanging on. I stumble backward, unsteady in the sand. I land on my butt with a grunt.

Mayor Morgan looks back at me with a scowl and murmurs something to the officer he's speaking to before coming back to me. "You can't listen to a thing I tell you. Can you? Let's go. I'm taking you home, then you're staying there while I deal with this mess."

"I can walk."

"Can you?"

I close my lips over the argument I want to make. The anger in his eyes tells me he won't listen to a thing I say. I've broken his trust for the last time, so nothing I say will be heard. My knees give out on me while I try to stand. Dad grips my arm to help my next attempt.

Someone in an EMT uniform rushes over to talk to my father. He tells them that he's taking me home, then he'll be right back. At this point, the police are pushing back the gawking tourists. My entire body shakes, and my heart feels like it's going to burst through my rib cage at any moment. My morning of peace is anything but what I wanted from it.

The EMT runs back to the other emergency personnel. Father grabs my arm and drags me across the sand. I stumble along without protest, wanting to be away from the carnage as quickly as possible. Another glance at the ocean shows me a familiar shimmer that makes me shiver.

Dad's car waits for us just on the other side of the boardwalk. He opens the door, shoving me in while trying to only look concerned. All the spectators will keep him in check for now. Once in the car, all bets are off. This is going to be a very uncomfortable ride home, but at least I'm away from the body leaving blood soaking into the sand.

Chapter Nineteen
Consequences

Before he can start ripping me a new one, Dad's phone rings. "Mayor Morgan. I'll be back as soon as I drop my daughter off. Are you sure? Well, make sure to clear the beach and start the investigation. Yes. I understand. Thank you."

He hangs up and tosses his phone into the center console with a half-finished coffee and pieces of donut. The muscle in his jaw ticks. I look out the window to keep from staring at it. I'm not sure if he's thinking or waiting until he's far enough away to not be noticed yelling at me as easily. Either is fine with me. The longer we put this conversation off, the better.

Dad takes a deep breath. "Why do you hate me?"

"I didn't hate you until you destroyed the last thing my mother ever gave me," I answer with a sigh, my gaze still watching the buildings go by.

"You've never obeyed me."

"Disobedience isn't the same as hate. Obedience doesn't equal love. If you think so, you're confused."

Silence stretches for a few agonizing moments before he finally speaks again. "You're grounded."

I turn back to meet his gaze, which is stormy with the force of contained rage. "I'm nineteen."

"I don't care. You are still grounded. You lost your allowance and free roaming privileges. I'm tired of you putting yourself in danger."

"I wasn't in danger."

"Did you not see what just happened?!"

My eyes desperately want to roll, but I hold the expression back to keep from pushing him further over the edge. "I never go into the water."

"Things can still get you while you're dry."

I shrug. At this point, I don't think I can find it in myself to care. My eyes turn back to the window. "If something would have happened, you wouldn't need to worry about my defiance anymore."

"That's not in the least bit funny."

"I wasn't trying to be."

I'm not sure what's wrong with me. Anger and fear should be my default emotions. I should be raging against him for trying to ground an adult. I should be shaking from what I just saw happen. Instead, I'm carrying on a conversation in an emotionless voice and looking out the window as if the world is no different today than it was yesterday.

"I feel numb," I mumble.

Dad must hear because he takes a deep breath and tries again. "I'm trying to protect you from the evil in this world."

"He talked to me," I say instead of reacting to his statement. It's not like I haven't heard it before, so it means very little to me.

"What?"

"I was sitting on the sand, singing. He walked up to tell me I have a beautiful voice."

"The man who died?"

I nod. "Yes, then he tried to get me to go somewhere with him, and I had to fight to get away."

I can almost hear Father's muscles tense further. If he keeps this up, he won't be able to move with how stiff he'll be. Silence is heavy, but it expresses so much emotion that I swear the heat increases inside our small space. I sit and wait, thinking of nothing but the bright sun in the blue sky. It's a pretty day.

"This is why I keep you home, Naomi. He could have seriously hurt you," Dad says after a few deep breaths.

"Do you know what you sound like?"

"What?" He sounds tired now.

"The world's worst helicopter parent."

"Damn it, Naomi. This is serious."

"So am I," I reply. "You can't protect us forever. You didn't take us under your wing; you chained us beneath it with a weight that keeps us from breathing. We won't know how to react to the real world with how sheltered you force us to be."

"There are worse things out there than being sheltered."

I sigh. "Like being eaten alive in the ocean."

"Naomi!"

"Sorry. I don't feel right."

I don't. What happened keeps playing over and over in my head. Where is the horror I felt on the beach? Where is the fear? Where are any of my emotions?

Dad sighs. "Punishment stands. That call was to tell me to have lunch before I return. They're investigating now and will have ideas and documents for me to sign when I return. This is an emergency, but they are more worried about you for witnessing it. You looked shell-shocked on the beach."

"And you're not?"

"I warned you not to go."

I laugh, but there's no amusement in it. "All-seeing mayor. Knows when someone is going to be eaten and tells his daughters to stay away."

"This is getting us nowhere."

"True."

"We will continue this conversation when the shock wears off."

"Can't wait."

Dad growls, but I'm still watching the blurs outside my window. The look on his face is lost to me. I wonder if he's scowling and clenching his hands on the steering wheel. I would bet my life on the fact that he is. I couldn't care less right now.

We pull into the driveway. Dad gets out, and we walk in together—me a few steps behind him and still not feeling anything. A couple of heads look up at our entrance. Wicked gleams twinkle when they see me, but they fall when they see our father with me. Clara smirks. Something else I don't care about.

Sandwiches are easy to make, even when barely seeing the world. He sits at the table with me, eating in silence but watching me for any sign of my usual defiance. All I can do is look at my food. My stomach feels as numb as my mind does.

"You don't need to worry about me going back to the beach. Not after what I just saw," I whisper.

He pauses, half-chewed bite mouthful in full view with his jaw hanging. I poke my bread to make an indent in the fluffiness, then do it a few more times. How can he eat right now? Does he see so many horrors that he's oblivious to the insanity of it all?

"That doesn't stop you from being grounded." I can hear the suspicion in his voice.

"I'd never dream of expecting otherwise. I just thought you'd like to know. How long am I grounded?"

"Until I feel I can trust you."

It doesn't matter. It's not like I have somewhere to be, so the question doesn't make sense to me, even though I am the one that asked it. I'll stay a homebody and wallow in my protective custody.

"I don't want to see it again," I say with another poke of bread. "The screams were horrendous. There was so much blood. He was still alive when they pulled him out of the boat. Not even a creep deserves that. What did that to him?"

When the silence stretches, I see an unsettled look on his face. He's staring at the sandwich halfway to his mouth, but even from this angle, the expression gives me chills.

"Dad?"

He visibly shakes himself. "Sorry, I was lost in thought. That scene was horrific. It was probably a shark. This isn't the first incident recently. A boy lost his leg a week or two ago."

Oh, yeah. I'm not supposed to know about that. Keeping my mouth shut about that subject might be in my best interest right now. If Dad knew I witnessed both attacks, he'd go even more berserk and paranoid.

The need to say it didn't look like a shark struggles for freedom. I'm able to force it down and keep it hidden. This is an argument I don't need. I'm just glad I'm not being screamed at. He seems more subdued than usual, which doesn't take much. Travis Morgan does not let anything subdue him.

"I'm not hungry," I say, standing to toss my sandwich away.

"I need to get back to the investigation. I mean it when I tell you not to let me find you outside the property again, particularly at the beach."

"Wouldn't dream of it."

Dad looks suspicious, but I turn to return my plate. He's not done, so I pause by the doorway. "If you listen to me in this, I'll make the grounding last only a few days. We can start small. I'm not unreasonable, Naomi."

I nod for an answer, walk into the kitchen to throw my sandwich away, and make my way to my room. For once, the curiosity my sisters contain is enough to keep their mouths shut and their thoughts of bullying and annoyance hidden. I close the door behind me.

As soon as I'm alone, I lean my back against the door and let my emotions take over. I'm not sure where they were before, but I'm glad they waited for the relative privacy of my room to return. Sobbing, I slide down the smooth wood until I'm sitting on the floor with my back against the solid surface. I cry and gasp, using my hands over my mouth to keep my wails muffled. Visions of blood and guts flash over me, and I find myself curling into a ball on the floor.

When the distress runs its course, I feel empty once more. I lie on my carpet for a bit and just breathe. Once I stop shaking, I stand on trembling legs and wobble my way to the bathroom. A hot shower; that's what I need. That's what I give myself.

I let the steam wash away the filth I feel covered in. I know I wasn't close to the body, but I feel soiled all the same. Once I step out, I realize my phone is ringing and hurry over to answer.

"Hey, Naomi. It's Stephen."

I startle, slowly remembering his promise to call me back. "Oh, hey, Stephen."

"Are you alright?"

"Yeah. Why wouldn't I be?"

"Because you sound a little upset."

Damn it. I was hoping the shower would calm me enough to hide my emotions. It apparently didn't. Despite all my bravado about not actually breaking the promise, I don't feel like testing that with Stephen. "Nothing important. Just an argument with my father."

"Okay. So, I promised to give you more information. Are you able to talk?"

I settle on my bed, ready for a bunch of talk of magical beings I refuse to believe in. "Yep."

"A mermaid took my sister."

He pauses to let it sink in, and I find my back stiffening. "I'm so sorry."

"She found a scale one day on the beach. She thought it was beautiful and carried it everywhere with her. Then she started to have nightmares about drowning in open air and started craving meat, mainly seafood, when she used to hate it. Imagine hating seafood while living next to the sea."

I give a sad smile that he can't see. "I couldn't imagine. I've always loved seafood. That love has become a little more..."

"Intense?"

"Yeah."

"Every time she went to the beach, she couldn't breathe unless she was touching water, so she stopped going for a while. She didn't tell me everything because I think she thought I'd believe she was crazy, but I didn't. I put enough together to try to save her."

"But you couldn't?"

When silence greets my question, I flinch at how heartless I probably sound. I'm sure he probably feels a lot of grief still, and I probably added guilt to that. I'm an idiot. Well, I never said I was good at social interactions. That doesn't mean I don't feel bad for saying it.

"I'm sorry," I say when the silence stretches too long. "I didn't mean it like that. It's just... This is all so hard for me to wrap my head around. Mermaids are myths."

"It's okay," he says after a moment. "The death of a loved one is not something you tend to get over. It's still raw. And I understand your hesitation to believe."

"No one else on that site does."

"They're idiots. The problem is, I'm having trouble deciding how to make you believe. I'm not sure how to save your life if you won't admit the truth behind mermaids."

I purse my lips and fall back on my bed with a sigh. "Why don't you tell me what happened to your sister?"

"Not much more to tell. She admitted that she noticed physical changes when she came in contact with the ocean, but she never elaborated on it. Other stories filled in some of those blanks. When I finally made myself believe in the unbelievable, I realized she had to stay away from the ocean. I went to tell her, but she was already missing."

"She went to the beach?"

He's quiet for a few more moments. His voice is soft whenever he speaks again. "Yes. I was too late. I tried to call her, and she answered. The sound of waves crashing came through the phone. Begging her did no good because she told me it felt like the sea was calling to her. The entire time, the sounds of the waves grew louder. I jumped in my car and raced out. Halfway, she stopped talking. When I got there, she was already gone."

Stephen's voice breaks at the end. I'm silent for a bit, mulling over everything he just told me and giving him a moment to compose himself. It's clear to me that he really loved his sister and wished that he could have convinced her to stay.

"But if you didn't see it happen..." I say, unable to hold it back.

"I ran onto the dock. There, I saw a glimmer in the water. Unsure what it was, I watched. It came closer to me."

My heart stops. "Do you know what it was?"

"It was her. When they want to be seen, they release their magic enough to let those they want to see be able to. I know this because when the shimmer came close, her head popped out of the water. Except, it wasn't completely her."

I don't think I've taken a breath since my last question, so I suck in as much air as possible to get enough oxygen for my next one. "What do you mean?"

"She had gills on her chest. When she smiled at me, her teeth were sharp and needle thin. I think she was smiling to tell me not to worry about her, but she didn't speak. She left, splashing her tail out of the water to dive deeper. It was pink and orange, covered in scales. There's nothing else she could have been. She was a mermaid."

My mind goes over what he just told me, and I try to figure out if I told him details about my hallucinations. I don't think I did, but how else could he know? Grasping onto one piece of information he gave me that I can, I say, "But I don't have to be near the ocean."

Okay, so I may have given him confirmation that the same thing is happening to me. I wince when I realize I've given it away, but why would it matter when he already knows so much? I need reassurance more than anything else right now.

"You don't?" he asks.

"No. I've had things that I think are hallucinations happen in my bathroom. I've never had anything happen like that at the beach."

Stephen asks me for more information, so I give in and tell him everything. If I'm crazy, so is he. Maybe we can be committed together, babbling about magical sea creatures.

"I don't know," he says after some thinking, "but what you've said fills in a few blanks my sister left. Please, Naomi."

When he stops, I find myself tensing. "What?"

"No matter what happens in your bathroom or how strong of an urge you get to go to the beach, stay away from the ocean."

I gulp at the urgency in his voice, which is understandable after what he told me. Too bad I've already been there multiple times since I found the scale. Nothing has happened to me when I went though. Although I can't speak about that fact when it comes to others. I also haven't touched the water. What if this isn't all some kind of insanity? Maybe I'm finally starting to believe.

Chapter Twenty
Coming Storm

I've managed to avoid the beach for the last five days. It hasn't been easy because with every day away from the ocean, I feel an increasing aching desire to hear the waves and smell the water. Crazy enough, I also feel the need to dip my feet in the tide. All of that feels like stupidity.

Every time the craving gets almost overwhelming, I call Stephen. He answers every call, even if he's working. It seems that he is taking his failure to save his sister seriously and wants to make up for it with me. I won't argue. So far, he's been able to talk me down every single time.

Through these conversations, I've also learned that he lives where he is now to get as far from any coast as he can possibly get. Anything to stay away from the mermaids. Last time, I asked him if it's only women they take. He told me men have been taken as well, but it doesn't happen as often. Mermaids find something they like too much in the human to let them go, so I can't hope that this one gets bored with me.

That makes me doubtful because I'm not some special beauty or anything. What could a mythical creature see in me that makes him want to steal me away to his underwater home? There's nothing special about me. Don't these fantasy creatures collect beautiful things? I'm far from beautiful.

Stephen doesn't believe these arguments and tries to tell me it's the call of the ocean making me doubt and say these things about myself, but it's not. I've always felt this way. Many of my sisters are gorgeous. I'm a bit lackluster compared to them. He doesn't believe me.

Sighing, I stare out the window in front of my desk, book forgotten in front of me. My concentration has been absolutely nonexistent lately. I'm not sure if it's because I want so badly to feel the water on my toes or if it's the lack of sleep due to increasing nightmares. I won't even mention the hallucinations that I'm starting to believe are real. They're not progressing anywhere, and I've only seen scales in the bath. I refuse to do more than take a quick shower anymore.

I miss bubble baths.

Everything that I love, everything that relaxes me, has been stolen away from me, leaving me a mess of need and brain fog. Mornings at the beach are out of the question, even if I'm still trying to wrap my head around everything and decide if I believe it, because it's not worth the risk. Bathing makes me scale over. Reading is impossible when I have to reread the same paragraph five times. People die when I go near the sand.

There's not much left for me. I've gone back to being the dutiful daughter, and Father has revoked my *grounding*. Every meal is torture because I have no way to smooth out the sharp edges caused by the stress of dealing with my family. Something must break soon, and I'm afraid of what will happen when it does.

The desire to go to the beach spikes to the point I find myself halfway to my door before noticing. Blinking, I'm able to stop myself. I take a few deep breaths to fight the pull to continue to my doom. My hands shake as I dig my phone out of my pocket. I hate bothering Stephen so much, but if he expects me to keep my promise, it's up to him to help me do it.

I scroll until I find his name in my contacts, considering that it might be pertinent to add him to my favorites, but a knock interrupts my resolve to call. Shaking hands stuff my phone back into my pocket, and I open the door. All stress is suddenly forgotten.

"Emma!" I've never been this excited. I throw my arms around her in a hug, the first one I think I've ever given one of my sisters. She grunts and laughs. "You're okay."

Emma pushes me away with a smile. "Of course I am. I finally found a sister I like. I'm not going to give that up because of a silly accident."

Darkness clouds her eyes, but she shakes it away. I'm sure I understand what killed the mood. It's hard to joke about a car accident that put you and your sister into commas and killed the driver. I've managed to ignore the guilt and self-loathing, but the dark cloud still hovers above me.

I step away from the door and motion for her to come in. "How are you feeling?"

"Tired and still a bit sore, but well enough. How are you?"

"Nothing physical."

Nothing related to the accident.

"You must heal fast. While I feel better, there are times I still feel like I've been run over by a bus."

Nodding, I give her my chair, so she has a back to rest against. I take the bed. We talk a bit about the craziness she's missed while not being home. When things grow quiet, I think the conversation has run its course.

It seems Emma is simply trying to come up with a way to broach the next subject. "I heard about the fatality at the beach and that you were there."

Flinching, I look down at my hands, which start shaking again. I take a few deep breaths. Once again, the incident has been ruled a shark attack. I've never seen a shark do that. What can I do? Tell them a mermaid did it?

"How did you find out?" I ask.

"Lucy called to tell me. She's been keeping me in the know about huge things, which isn't often. Bickering sisters aren't newsworthy events. Deaths my sister was at are. She told me Dad grounded you."

I nod. "Yeah. He warned me the next time he found out about my beach trips, he'd remove my allowance privileges. He added the grounding because of what I witnessed, I think."

The fact that he accosted me before he died is something I'm not going to tell her about. Whenever I think too hard about it, I worry that it's my fault and feel guilty. I'm not sure how it's my fault, but my mind won't stop nagging me about it. That's a shadowy darkness I don't want to spiral into.

"He grounded you and took away your only means of cash because you witnessed something traumatic? That's a bit backwards," Emma says.

"He warned me about my disobedience."

"But you were traumatized!"

A dark chuckle escapes me. "That is less important than his reputation and my disobedience."

"Bastard," she mumbles under her breath. I jump at the sentiment, which makes her shrug. "He is. We got the father of the year, didn't we?"

"You can say that."

Emma sighs. "You're still going, right?"

My head jerks to meet her gaze. "I've already lost my allowance and have been grounded. A nineteen-year-old... grounded..."

"So? I can help you buy the things you need. It's no big deal. The beach is everything to you."

I grimace and look away. "Not anymore. Not after what happened."

My chair creaks as Emma stands. She sits next to me on the bed and grabs my hand. "I know what you witnessed is terrible, and I understand how it might make you want to avoid the beach. But I also know that the ocean is an integral part of who you are. You can't give that up."

What does she want me to say? So many bad things have happened when I've gone there. It's not just the death that I'm sure was murder. It's not like I can tell her that a mermaid is stalking me and killing people and animals at the beach. Every time I go there, something bad happens. I have enough on my conscience.

"I can't," is all I say, and I do that in a whisper.

"Naomi, you'll feel better if you don't change who you are. I can go with you."

I flinch, not wanting her to witness the things my mere presence causes and might put her in danger. "Maybe I just need more time."

My kind sister takes a deep breath. "Maybe you do. Here, I'll run you a bath to relax in."

I tense, and I can't tell her the real reason behind it. "You don't have to. I can run my own."

I'm thankful when she misreads the tension. "Nonsense. They discharged me because I'm better. I can do this much for you."

Further protests won't work, so I watch her walk into my bathroom and start running water. The scent of lavender permeates the air, telling me she added my relaxing bubble bath. My heart skips a beat at the thought of her making me get in the water.

When it's done, I'm still sitting on the bed, my hands fisting my comforter. Emma walks out with a smile. "All full. I'll leave, so you can strip and soak. If you need anything at all, let me know. It doesn't matter what it is."

She slips out. Instead of standing, I stare at the bathroom doorway in horror. Emma just got home and went through all the trouble of drawing a bath. Standing, I slowly walk into the bathroom as if the water is going to jump up and bite me. The only time the bathtub doesn't cause this kind of intense reaction is when I'm getting in it to stop suffocating; like that doesn't sound insane. Soaking always brings scales. I'm afraid of what might happen if I keep doing it.

Kneeling, I reach in and pull the plug. She doesn't need to know that her effort went unused. I can thank her later and tell her it made me feel better. She needs to know I appreciate her. That doesn't mean I'm willing to turn into a mermaid for her.

With that thought, the desire to go to the beach picks up again. This time, I'm able to make my call. Stephen answers, knowing exactly what I need. He avoids all talk of water and mermaids. Instead, he tells me what stupid things his roommate has done over the years, which keeps me laughing until the urge to sabotage myself disappears. Knowing he's at work, I thank him and hang up.

The sky outside my window grows dark. It's mid-afternoon, so I know what that means. My backyard is the only place outside I feel safe anymore, so I head out to get some peacefulness—the little that I can.

As soon as I reach the backyard, the wind picks up, bringing dampness to my face. I stiffen up but force the alarm down. It's only impending rain. I can't let myself be afraid of all water. Stephen says it's saltwater that will trigger my ultimate change. He doesn't know what the bath does to me because our calls are about calming the raging need inside of me. Talking about what happens when I'm submerged in any water for an extended time would do the opposite.

Maybe I should tell him. The information might give him more to go on. He tells me he's researching more on my situation, which makes me laugh because how do you research something like this? It's not like it's a well-studied topic. Who would believe in it enough to study it?

I sit on the picnic bench, my back against the table. I lift my face to the breeze and force the anxiety the dampness causes down. Rain and humidity aren't scary. My baths and the beach won't take this much from me. I inhale deeply and take in the scent of the incoming storm. Thunder crashes in the distance, probably still over the ocean. That doesn't matter. Storms travel fast here.

Abigail yells out the backdoor to remind me that it's my turn to help cook. I nod without looking to let her know I hear. Cooking supper is the last thing I feel like doing today, but I have to pretend to be the dutiful daughter until I can have my allowance reinstated and get the hell away from the coast. I only hope I can last that long.

"Naomi."

The sound of my name from the opposite side of the yard tenses my shoulders. The familiar voice makes my teeth clench. Why is she here? Why can't she let me be? I want nothing to do with her or her creepiness.

My eyes drop from the sky to find hers as she steps out from behind our pink tree. It figures Lenora would come on the edge of a storm. I scowl, unable to hide my displeasure at her presence. The annoying woman only smirks.

"I haven't seen you at the beach lately, Naomi. Has something happened?"

Chapter Twenty-One
Hopelessness

Lightning flashes in the dark sky, brightening Lenora's dark hair momentarily and making her eyes almost glow. Pink petals fall around her as if something out of a fantasy. The smile she flashes me is colder than the light mist that saturates the air now. I shiver and look away. I've already thought she was creepy, but the storm isn't helping. It's more than just the feeling she gives me in this backdrop.

"I've been going, even if I don't see how it's your business," I say once the thunder subsides.

"Testy, Ms. Morgan. It was a simple question. Besides, you haven't been there recently. I've been watching for you."

I try to make my laugh sound convincing, but it sounds hollow, even to me. "It's a big beach, Lenora. Whether I go or not is not a concern you need to worry about."

She strides past the pale tree trunk and further into the yard. The look in her eyes sends chills over me. I see anger and annoyance there. I've pissed her off somehow. It can't be from not going to the beach because that has no consequence to her. The need to hug myself in her presence creeps up on me, but I do my best to ignore it and push it down.

Right now, Lenora is looking at me like a predator drooling over prey. Prey that shows weakness doesn't live very long. I must keep myself calm and act like it doesn't matter that she showed up. I'm not scared of her. There are bigger things on my plate right now.

"It's obvious that something is bothering you. I've noticed you on the beach almost every morning long before we met face to face. You have a very beautiful voice, Naomi Morgan."

I scrape my teeth across my bottom lip before I realize I'm doing it. It's a movement that speaks volumes, so I force myself to stop. Calm and collected. The fact that she has been watching me for so long sends an unpleasant shiver over me that I hope she takes as a byproduct of the chilly drizzle starting. No weakness. No opportunity to pounce.

"It seems I'm at a disadvantage," I say, trying to make it seem like I couldn't care less. It's hard when every muscle of my body screams at me to run into the house. "I didn't know I was being watched."

"I wasn't stalking you if that's what you're concerned about. Mornings at the beach are peaceful. It makes for easy planning and contemplation of the past. I do it often. Your voice makes it even easier."

"Well, I'm glad you find solace in my singing, but it was rude not to make yourself known. If you don't have anything important to say, I have a supper to help cook."

She doesn't need to know that I have fifteen or twenty minutes before that becomes a problem. Anything to make her go away. When Lenora doesn't take the hint, I begin to consider walking backwards toward the house. That might do the opposite of what I want right now. I'm not scared of her. She has nothing to use against me.

"Rude or not, I've missed it," she says.

My jaw clenches. Why can't this woman take a hint? I bought a single jewelry box off of her. It's not like we were ever best friends. We were never even worst friends. She's delusional if she thinks otherwise. It was supposed to be a single transaction. The recurring run-ins and repeated gifts are becoming too much.

"Not that it's any of your business, but I simply haven't felt like going." That may be a bit rude, but my annoyance is rising to the level my father usually sports around me. She needs to go away. Besides, I'm long past caring if I hurt the feelings of someone that just won't leave me alone.

"Is it the death you witnessed?"

The breath is forced out of my lungs in a loud whoosh, as if I've been hit in the chest with a sledgehammer. My feet force me to take a step back as the shock fully registers. After what she said about the boy who lost his leg, I don't want to know her thoughts on the murder-slash-shark-attack. How does she even know I was there?

As if she can read my thoughts, Lenora's face is devoured in a devious smirk. "I know all that happens near the sea, my dear. Did you know it was a gift for you?"

"What are you even talking about?"

"He hurt you or threatened you in some way before losing his life? Am I right? The ocean protects what it wants."

I bite my tongue with a wince. "You aren't putting his death on me. That wasn't my fault."

She cocks her head to the side. Another rumbling thunder rolls through the sky. The look in her eyes looks downright evil when the lightning flashes again. Screw not showing weakness; I take another step back.

The gloating in her expression is even worse. What makes her triumphant about the death of a man? Glee shouldn't be anywhere near her eyes, but it's shining bright there. I gulp and take yet another step toward safety.

"Everything you do has consequences," Lenora says. "That's something your father never understood. Curse for a curse. Blood for blood. If you don't face your mistakes, who knows who will be the one to pay for them?"

"What the hell are you talking about?!"

This time, my foot hits a small hole when I take another step back. I stumble, taking my eyes off Lenora to make sure I don't twist my ankle again. When I look, she's gone. There's no sign of her presence at all. Only the laughter I'm sure I'm imagining in my head.

"Naomi, what the hell are you doing out here? It's storming. Do you want to be struck by lightning?"

Startled, I spin to face the house and almost twist my ankle anyway. Dad stands on the deck. It's not until I view him through a curtain of water that I realize it's pouring down rain. My distress must've hidden that fact from me.

"I'll come in," I say in a voice that shakes enough to narrow my father's eyes.

As I try to walk past him, he reaches out and grabs my arm. "What's going on?"

"Nothing, Dad. I swear. I thought I saw something in the bushes. It scared me, but it turned out to be only a groundhog."

His eyes stare at me with suspicion. "You weren't trying to find some way to run off without me knowing?"

The thought that he might know even my most secret plans makes my heart stop. "No."

"I won't have you at the beach again, Naomi."

My heart starts again. It's not about my plans to run away. He just thinks I'm trying to get back to the place he's forbidden me. I do my best to keep that relief to myself. "No, Dad. After what I saw, I have no wish to go back there."

The tension in his shoulders melts away, making me curious about just what he expects to happen to me. I can handle myself. There is usually someone else around if needed. The fact that Lenora is the one always around makes me shiver.

Dad tenses again. "What's wrong now?"

I do my best to shrug nonchalantly. "I think I'm just cold. I am soaking wet."

"That will teach you to stand out in the middle of a storm. If you get sick, stay in your room. You don't need to get your sisters ill through your stupidity."

Thanks a lot for your care, father dear.

"I'm sure I'll be fine, but I really should get some dry clothes on. My teeth will be chattering soon."

Dad lets go of my arm. "Very well. Get dry and come back down. I saw you are part of the cooking group today."

Nodding with a fake smile, I slip past him and into the kitchen. They're already starting, but I ask them to give me a minute to change before heading through the dining room and up the stairs. Lucy is cleaning her books and notes from the table as I go by, so I flash her a real smile. It's long past time I gave the couple of sisters that are worth anything the regard they deserve.

In the living room I pass at the base of the stairs, Brooke is complaining about the paint Emma got on the carpet. They're about to start arguing. I rush past before I can get roped in. Emma doesn't need my back-up. I'd give it to her if needed. Although, that would make me late for supper, and I'd have to deal with Dad's ire.

Upstairs, I rush to my room and stop inside once the door is closed. I take a few deep breaths to calm myself, proud I was able to hide my raging emotions from my family. The safety of my room gives me the space to sob away the fear and frustration I feel. I'm not sure what is wrong with Lenora, but she needs to let whatever vendetta she has against my family go. Her last words tell me there is one, and I have absolutely nothing to do with what happened.

After a few more deep breaths, I walk into the bathroom, peel my wet clothes off of me, and hang them on the towel racks. I then hop into the shower with the water as hot as I can stand it. I wasn't completely lying to Dad; my entire body is frozen to the point I'm starting to feel numb.

It only takes a minute or two to warm up enough, then I move back out to grab some sweatpants and a hoodie. This should keep me warm—hopefully, not too much. I towel my hair dry and return to my bathroom to hang that up as well.

As I leave the bathroom, I'm hit by a wave of dizziness. Gasping, I grab the door frame to steady myself and avoid a nasty fall. The strong thirst—an unavoidable need for water—comes over me. Knowing what comes next, I stumble back toward the bathtub. The suffocation comes before I can take more than a step onto the tile.

This time, it hits so hard, my vision darkens in seconds. I try to cry for help, but I can't speak. I can't breathe. I can't see. Stumbling, I try to force myself toward the tub, but I estimate that I only make it halfway before my knees give out on me. Tearing fabric echoes through the room, followed by the horrendous itching I know too well for my own comfort.

Sobbing without sound or air, I feel my thighs, fused down to my knees. The familiar feeling of scales meets my hesitant fingers. I try desperately to crawl to the tub. Anything for the relief I need. My lungs are burning. My heart pounds so hard that it echoes in my ears. Every part of my body is struggling.

Pulling my useless legs along with tired arms, I find the side of the tub. I try to lift myself up to the edge and fall back to the floor. Rage makes me want to scream, but I know I can't even do that much. Whatever takes over me keeps me from crying out for help every time. It's useless to even wish for my voice.

Frantic fingers grasp at the edge of the tub. When they curl around it, I want to yell in triumph. That's not possible right now either. I find the lever for the faucet through the haze covering my vision. The sound of water makes me feel hopeful, then my other hand slips. My head hits the edge of the tub, bringing pain and bright flashes.

As I listen to the sound of water running down the drain, I feel the desire to just let go within me. I try to fight it, but I can't. Tears stream down the side of my face and onto the cool tile. Oblivion takes me, the sound of water slowly fading, accentuated by a knocking and a violent rumble of thunder. I hear my name. I'm too far gone to care. Blackness takes over.

Chapter Twenty-Two
Accusations

Familiar beeping grabs my attention from the black void I'm stuck in. This time, there are no nightmares to wake from with a start. Only black nothingness floats around my mind as it struggles back into consciousness. I feel like I'm floating on the air, even if I can't see around me. Well, I can't see air, so what does my sightlessness matter right now?

As time goes, small things catch my focus. Something warm and soft lying over me. Bright light outside the darkness. Overly strong aftershave that sparks memory that's too insubstantial to grasp. It flutters into the dark without enlightening me to what I should remember.

My breath hitches in my chest when I try to breathe deep. My toes twitch beneath the softness. A soft voice reaches my ears, gentle and careful. A louder one jars me closer to the brink of opening my eyes. Of course, that voice doesn't care if it wakes me, probably unhappy when I finally do.

Now, I'm stubbornly trying to hold on to the oblivion I once fought. This time, my mind tries to propel me toward consciousness that I no longer want. I resist as hard as possible, having no weapons to fight the inevitable. Despite my desires, my eyes flutter open.

"She's waking," the kind voice says.

The gruff voice replies with, "About time."

Bright likes make me suck in a deep breath, but consciousness comes back quickly. "Where am I?"

My voice is only a whisper, but Lucy is sitting close enough to hear it. "The ER, Naomi. We found you unconscious on your floor."

I wince, the real world rushing back to me. Like the other times sleeping on my floor, the blurriness disappears as fast as it came. I feel fit to get out of bed and move around. Cautious, I look at my father by moving only my eyes. Maybe if I don't move my head, he won't notice. He's not looking at me, so maybe he missed the interaction. Of course, that's too big of a hope to come true.

"What happened to you?" he asks with a low growl coiled in his deep voice.

Memories of the pain and suffocation, my desperation to reach the bathtub, and the uselessness of my body flash through my mind. Squeezing my eyes shut, I try my best to push them down. I don't want to remember my latest mermaid episode. Then I remember the feeling of scales and the discomfort of my thighs molding together.

Gasping, my eyes fly open, and I look at my bare legs beneath the blankets. The hospital gown rides up to my hips, revealing smooth legs covered in skin—two of them. I part my knees to test how separate they are. A relieved breath whooshes out of me when my legs part without issue.

"Clara came to get me when you didn't show up to help cook supper," Dad says. I'd roll my eyes at the predictability of my tattle-tail sister if I wasn't partly grateful for it. "I sent Lucy up to get you. She found you on the floor with your pants torn in two beside you. What the hell happened?"

"I don't fully remember," I tell him as truthfully as I can. That's not a lie. I have memories, but everything still feels fuzzy.

"Did someone break in and assault you?"

My brow furrows at the question. "Who would have been able to get into the house?"

"Well, what else am I supposed to believe? You told me someone tried to assault you at the beach. Maybe his friends followed you home."

Lucy gasps, making me wince. "You were assaulted?"

I huff. "No."

"That's not what you told me, Naomi," our father says. "Or was that a lie to make your infraction seem smaller?"

I scoff. "I didn't lie or exaggerate. I wasn't assaulted. Being accosted doesn't immediately mean assaulted. It was too open on the beach. If he wanted to assault me, he would have needed to lure or drag me to the place he suggested we go. It didn't happen, so I wasn't assaulted. Believe it or not, I'm smart enough to not allow a strange man to lure me away without a fight. I'm no longer the child you treat me as."

I'm not sure why the difference matters so much to me. There's no doubt in my mind the man would have if given the chance. He was certainly interested and trying. Like I said, I'm not dumb enough to follow an unknown man, whether Dad believes that or not.

"But he would have?" Lucy asks.

A glance at her worried eyes makes me wince. Maybe that's why it matters. I don't want to concern the only two people in this world that worry about me. Three, if you include Stephen, but I'm not because it's not to save me. He simply wants to assuage his guilt over the loss of his sister. The man in the room with me only cares as much as my actions affect him.

"But he didn't," I say. "It's done and in the past. It's not like he can hurt anyone anymore anyway."

I flinch at the coldness the final statement makes me feel. Sure, the man was an asshole and a predator, but I shouldn't make it sound like I'm glad he's dead. I now feel heartless.

"What do you mean?" Lucy asks.

"She means it was the man that later became a shark casualty," Father cuts in.

Lucy gasps and covers her mouth. I try not to roll my eyes at our father. Lucy may think it's her reaction that earned the disrespectful expression from me. Awkward silence takes over the cramped space. Although, any space containing Mayor Morgan is too cramped for me. Looking at my hand to avoid glancing at either of them, I pick at some dirt beneath one of my nails.

After a few more minutes of silence, our father snarls. "Why is it taking so long for the doctor to come back? He said they'd have the results of your blood test shortly, and that was two hours ago. Lucy, go see what's keeping them."

I tense at the thought of being in this room alone with Dad, but he doesn't say anything. His expensive shoe taps on the tiled floor to express his annoyance. There's a cap from a syringe under his chair, probably missed the box on the wall. Focusing on this little puzzle keeps my mind occupied to avoid saying something that'll make things worse.

Lucy comes back in and timidly takes her seat while looking at the hands clasped in her lap. Dad looks at her expectantly. When he becomes annoyed enough about her silence, he opens his mouth to berate her.

The doctor entering interrupts what he wanted to say. "Sorry for the wait, Mr. Morgan. Good to see you awake, Naomi."

I offer a stiff smile. Dad slips into his dutiful father persona and wins the doctor over with a fake happy expression that fools everyone. Again, I try not to roll my eyes. At this point, I just want out of this room.

"Can I go home?" I ask before the doctor can launch into whatever he came in to say.

He purses his lips. "We'd like another blood sample."

"Why?" Dad asks. "What's wrong with her blood?"

"We aren't sure. There are strange compounds floating around in her bloodstream that the lab can't isolate. It seems they first thought it was contaminated, like last time, but they don't feel that's what it is now. They tried to take a closer look, but the compounds dissolved before their eyes. We would like another look."

"What about all the levels you said you wanted to check?" Dad asks.

"They all appear to be normal, but we need a closer look at this strangeness in her blood. It could be the reason for her blackouts."

Father shoots me a look that would make me gulp if I didn't have control over my muscles. I do, so I only glare at him until he turns back to the doctor. "All her scans?"

My scans? How long have I been out? That's a stupid question. I usually pass out around bedtime and wake during early morning. I'm sure it's not that late. A glance at the clock says ten, but the windows are dark. Definitely not ten in the morning.

"Those all came back normal," the doctor says. "There is no apparent reason for her blackouts, so we need to explore all avenues."

"If everything is alright, we are heading home," Father argues.

The doctor turns to me because, in the end, it's my decision. Despite Dad's insistence otherwise, I am an adult with the right to answer for myself. My heart and body long for my bed. I'd do anything right now to be alone in the silence of my dark room. The look in Dad's eyes straightens my shoulders into defiance.

"How long would it take to get the results?" I ask the doctor.

"A few hours. You can go home after we take the blood."

"How long will that take?" Father asks after sending a scowl toward me.

"Not long. The nurse will need to come in, and I'll make sure she does it as soon as she's free. Then Naomi can sign the discharge papers after that."

The doctor walks out without waiting for Dad's reply. His face darkens, and I mentally add a point to my score. It feels like a competition over who has control of my free will. I refuse to lose that to him.

The silence is heavy and furious. I can tell Dad wants to express his displeasure, but he won't raise his voice in a public place. The fact that he's been less than agreeable in front of the doctor means he's already on edge. The car is free though, so that'll be fun. My only regret is Lucy is here to deal with it by my side. I'd spare her if I could.

Tapping noises fill the space again, more furious than last time. I can see the point that Father considers just dragging me out of here is worth considering when the nurse finally walks in. She takes three vials of blood and hands me the discharge papers to sign, then we're on our way. If the hospital wouldn't be full of so many witnesses, our father would probably grab our hands and run us to his car.

Once inside the vehicle, Dad starts the engine and pulls out before we even have our seatbelts on. He huffs, "What the hell is going on, Naomi?"

Ready to be yelled at for delaying him longer than necessary, I jerk in shock at the question I get instead. Lucy curls in on herself beside me in the back. My guilt that she has to be here right now rises again.

"I'm as clueless as you. I woke up in the hospital without any idea how I got there."

"Stop being so dramatic," he growls. "It's obvious that I would have called for an ambulance. The doctor talked like this isn't the first time."

"It's my first time in the ER over this."

"Stop hedging the questions. This isn't a game. How long have you been having blackouts?"

I sigh and look out the window at the lights blurring by. Water coats everything, but the storm is gone. "Since a little before the accident."

"And you didn't think to tell me?"

My hands clench and open on my lap a few times. I try to hold back but can't. "You're not exactly approachable. You'd probably say it was all my fault and accuse me of doing drugs."

"Are you?"

I laugh. "I'm the last daughter you need to be asking that."

"What's that supposed to mean?"

"Nothing but an expression to tell you what a stupid accusation that is."

"Well, what else am I supposed to suspect?"

The anger at his lack of care rises up. "Oh, I don't know, that maybe something is really wrong with your youngest offspring. That she needs compassion and help more than accusations and anger. I understand that's too much to ask for."

"Don't start with your attitude, Naomi."

"I'm tired of being treated like a criminal. I have no idea what's really wrong with me." Another half-lie.

"Stop acting like a criminal, and I'll stop treating you like one!"

Done with this conversation, I cross my arms over my chest and look out the window, my jaw set tight. I breathe out of my nose and keep my lips pressed together. I'm not a criminal. I'm not a druggie. I'm a lost and hated daughter that's turning into a freaking mermaid. He needs to get off my back.

CHAPTER TWENTY-THREE
URGES AND APPETITES

As I pull my hair out of its bun and step toward the shower, my phone buzzes. I stop and look to see a text from Stephen. I cannot deal with him this early in the morning. Not after the night I had. Leaving it unread, I step into the stream and try to wash the feeling of last night's hospital visit away. They already called to say that there are still traces of whatever is in my blood, but that it was fading. There's no point in giving more. I'm to go right to the hospital if I feel anything going on to have it checked at the start.

"Yeah, right?" I mutter into the water. "Like I'm going to let them see the weirdness my body becomes in the middle of it. I'll become nothing more than a science experiment."

My sigh sprays the water running over my face outward. Instead of dwelling, I focus my attention on scrubbing my skin off and stepping out of the shower. My phone starts ringing. It's Stephen.

Grunting, I silence the call, dry, and dress. As I'm brushing my hair, he calls again. I growl.

"Yes, Stephen."

"You didn't answer my text."

"I was in the shower," I say.

"I was worried you gave in. Are you mad at me?"

I grit my teeth and yank the brush through my last knot with a curse. "No. At least, not you specifically. I have a strange creepy woman stalking me. People and things get hurt or die around me. I'm turning into a freaking mermaid against my will, and I'm no Ariel. Random blackouts are becoming the norm. Well, maybe not random since they happen during changes that you tell me should only be happening near saltwater. I was in a car accident where me and my sister almost died, and one person did. I have a father who couldn't care less what happens to me as long as it doesn't embarrass him. Sisters that love to torment me. Then I was stuck in the hospital until late last night. Excuse me for not being Miss Sunshine."

Stephen is quiet on the other end, much to my relief. Maybe he'll leave me alone now. I'm tired of this whole mermaid business. If I ignore it, I can hope it'll just go away. How much I wish that was true.

"What do you mean, people and things keep getting hurt or dying around you?" he asks after a minute.

That's all he got from my rant? All that and he chooses the one that affects me least. I see where his priorities lie. The temptation to hang up on him grows strong. I take a moment to breathe through the rage. Of course, he cares about others. That doesn't mean he doesn't care about me as well. I'm just taking all my stress and frustration out on him.

Bless him, Stephen doesn't prod. He lets me sift through my raging emotions. I feel myself deflate.

"Fine," I say through a sigh. "The first time I went to the beach after I found the scale, I found a dead dog under the pier. It was water-logged, with maggots in its eyes and chunks missing. That same day, a boy that bumped into me with a football had his leg ripped off in the water. Later, I saw a whole dolphin pod slaughtered. Last time I was there..."

I pause. A promise to him means I shouldn't have been there that day. He senses my hesitation and prods this time. "The last time you were there..."

I want to yell at him for having expectations of me because I'm tired of living up to everyone else's expectations. The anger in me isn't strong enough to grasp a hold of. I take a deep breath. "I went the day after we talked for the first time."

"You promised me you wouldn't go."

"I promised not to go into the water."

Stephen groans. "That's an asinine deflection, and you know it. I'm not trying to be overbearing, Naomi. I'm only trying to help."

"I know," I say, drawing out the phrase. "My father was pushing my buttons about not listening to him, so I was tired of being told I couldn't do the one thing that brings me the most peace. I was angry."

"I get it. Believe it or not, I do. My parents were very controlling after my sister went *missing*. What happened that day?"

"Some guy came onto me and tried to get me to go somewhere secluded with him. I refused, but he wasn't taking no for an answer, so I had to forcefully get away. He was killed in the ocean not long after. Supposed shark attack."

"Both humans somehow had negative contact with you?"

That's Stephen—I'm learning this—not focusing on the present facts but looking for possible correlations. "Yes."

"Maybe the mermaid was taking revenge for you."

I laugh. "The first was barely anything. He just wasn't looking where he was going. Next, you're going to tell me the injury and death were gifts." He's quiet for too long. "Stephen?"

"Maybe they are."

"Come on!"

"Naomi, just bear with me," he says quietly into my ear. I can give him that much. "Maybe the dog was a gift as well. Sometimes animals leave food for those they care about. Then the dolphins may have been a tribute. It's possible that he would have given you some piece of that as well. The people were proof of his ability to defend you."

"You're sure it's a he?"

"Focus, Naomi."

I do, and I laugh again. "Next, you're going to tell me that the fish I found on the sand right before I found the scale and tooth was a tribute as well." When his silence greets me on the other end, I throw my head back and mouth silent curses at the ceiling. "You are, aren't you? I didn't even tell you that until right now."

"My mind works quickly. Is it too far to make sense?"

"No," I admit grudgingly. "How do I make him or her or it understand that I'm not interested and I don't want what they have to offer?"

"I'm not sure you can."

"That's not at all helpful, Stephen."

"This is so much different from my sister."

"Then maybe that's not what this is."

"You don't believe that, Naomi."

Being told what I believe annoys me, but I relent. "I don't."

"I'm going to reach out to some people and try to find more answers. Maybe these differences will help us head this off. The issue is, those I've talked to about it so far have had the same experience I did."

"So, I'm an anomaly."

"Exactly."

"You make that sound like a good thing," I say.

"It could be. Just keep holding on."

We say our farewells, and I decide to lose myself in a book. Again, my concentration isn't in it. The longer I fight the need to do something else, the more the craving for the sea returns. Not this again. Standing, I walk downstairs to get something to eat and drink. It's halfway between breakfast and lunch, but I'm not forced into sociable meals until supper. I can eat as I want until then.

I find breakfast burritos in the fridge and stare at them. Emma's voice makes me jump, banging my skull off the inside of the fridge. I pull my head out, rubbing the lump left from the refrigerator. "Oww."

Emma offers a softer smile. "Sorry, Naomi. I didn't know you were that engrossed. Lucy made breakfast burritos this morning. She's trying to soften up the tension between everyone, but I doubt it'll work. You're allowed to have one too. The ones marked S are sausage. The others are meatless."

A glance shows me the S that I missed during my first look. There's only one of those left. Oh well. I wasn't told I couldn't eat the last one. Lucy would probably tell me to anyway. I snatch the last sausage.

The toaster oven fills the kitchen with the smell of eggs, cheese, and sausage. I salivate at the thought of this meal. Emma offers me a blueberry, and I grimace at her.

She lifts an eyebrow. "You used to love fruit. Is everything alright?"

I turn away to flinch without adding concern to her questions. My desire for sugary goodies of every kind is low anymore. Too bad I know why now and can't explain it to her. She would never believe me. I can't say I blame her because I wouldn't believe her either if roles were reversed.

"I just haven't been in the mood lately," I say into my reflection on the toaster oven door.

"Are you pregnant?"

"What?" I say, jerk up and looking at her. When I see the thought she's putting into this question, I can't hold back a laugh. "Not even a chance. There is not a single guy in my life besides people I talk to online."

There. I let her know I have a virtual prospect—not that I consider Stephen a real prospect—while giving her the confirmation that there's no way I'm growing a life inside of me. None of it is a lie or even a half-truth. I try to reserve those for our wonderful father.

Her relief almost makes me laugh again. "I had to ask. Some of what you're describing can be pregnancy related."

"They'd be pretty extreme symptoms."

"You never know what might happen when hormones become unbalanced."

She has me there. "Trust me, if it happens, you'll be the first one I tell."

Another not lie because no one else will care. Lucy might, but I'd be afraid she'd tell Dad because of her meekness and her need to follow the rules. Emma nods and says she needs to get back to her latest painting. I give her a smile as she leaves.

Once the kitchen is empty, I chuckle again. Pregnant. That's a stretch, but I can see why she made it. If only that's what this is. Too bad it's not. I'd rather deal with my father's ire over an unexpected pregnancy than turning into a mermaid by force.

I take my warmed burrito upstairs, popping my head into Lucy's room to thank her, then sit at my desk to devour it. So good. The cheesy goodness and laughter over Emma's ideas about my health issues is enough to distract me from the pull of the ocean. Once that's done, I have nothing left to think about.

In an effort to provide more distraction, I take my plate down to wash it and circle the yard a few times. The fresh air actually makes the pull worse, so I retreat back into the stuffy house and up to my room. I rarely spend time in the other rooms of the house because my sisters are always sharing the space. At this point, I wonder if it might be a good idea. Even a negative distraction is still a distraction.

No. Lucy is probably studying. Emma is busy painting and doesn't need me to break her focus. The others are probably either gone or already fighting with each other. There will be no help there.

My heart aches with longing. Every time I stop thinking, I find myself facing the east, where the waves crash and call for me. I bite my lip and pull out my phone. Stephen is probably already tired of talking to me today with the crankiness he received earlier.

I have no other way to stop this. He picks up on the third ring. "Twice in one day. My lucky day." My silence kills his playfulness. "Naomi, what's wrong?"

"I'm sorry if you're working."

"Not today. I took a few days off."

"Why would you do that?"

I can almost hear the shrug in his voice. "Nothing big. I just needed the time. Are you alright?"

"My heart is calling for the beach."

He launches into antics and childhood stories without question. I hate relying on him, but I don't know how else to keep this urge at bay. I can't go to the beach. As much as I used to long for the freedom of the ocean, I've learned I don't really want it.

This time, his mindless conversation doesn't help. I think he realizes because he goes silent for a moment before saying, "Are you okay?"

I shake my head, fighting back tears. "I don't know."

"I know it's hard, Naomi. Try to push the feelings away. You can't go to the beach. Can you hold on?"

"I think so, but I don't know."

"Do what you can. I promise things will get better."

He doesn't say goodbye before hanging up this time. My body trembles with need that drives me back into the bathroom. I turn the shower on, not caring that I already took one. Clothes and all, I huddle

under the stream bursting from the faucet. I don't know what else to
do.

Chapter Twenty-Four
Unexpected Visitor

Bubbles tickle my forearm as I search for a piece of silverware in the hot water. Clara grimaces at her nails while wiping down all the cooking surfaces. Brooke scrapes stubborn food into the garbage as if it has wronged her. Abigail is in the dining room, wiping down the tables while Lucy vacuums the floor.

A fork stabs my finger, and I lift it to scrub with my sponge. The dish water is otherwise clear, so I start reaching for soaking pots. Once the dishes are done, I wipe the water off around the sink and wipe down the basin. My fingers are wrinkly by the time I dry my hands.

I grimace at the feeling of the skin on my hands and look around. Oily, yet rough. I hate it.

Everyone else is already done and gone. Brooke left the trash bag out but didn't take it to the bins. I groan. "Sure, I'll do it."

With a grunt, I lift the bag and waddle toward the door. Seven girls make a lot of trash. Although, I'm wondering if someone is trying to incriminate me by making me dispose of a body for them. This is heavy, and it wouldn't surprise me at this point.

Once outside, I have the two steps to the sidewalk that leads to the driveway to contend with. I make it with minimal grunting. Halfway to the driveway, I pause to breathe and wipe sweat from my forehead. Okay, there isn't a body in here; there's three. Seriously, what could my sisters possibly have that's this heavy? No wonder Brooke slipped out to make me do this. She must have lifted the bag and noped out of the kitchen while my back was turned. Typical.

While leaning down and panting with my hands on my knees, I hear someone else grunt and lift the bag. Startled, I look up to see a strange man I've never seen before. He looks to be about my age, maybe a few years older. Dark, unkempt hair fluffs over his head. Dark blue eyes smile down at me. Remembering the danger of the stranger at the beach, I take a wobbly step back.

"Where does this go?"

His deep voice triggers recognition. "Stephen? What the hell are you doing here?"

"Well, your reaction tells me I found the right girl. Where does this go?"

Glancing around to make sure no one has seen him, I lead him to the trash can with the barest thanks and drag him behind a tree at the end of our driveway. "Seriously, what are you doing here?"

"Helping take out the trash. What was in that anyway? Bricks?"

I rub my eyes and hold back my groan. "No. What are you doing here? You should be safe in your middle of the country hideaway."

"It seems that as long as I don't hurt you in the sight of it, I should be safe enough. Also, staying out of the water helps."

Even with his caution of not mentioning mermaids in the vicinity of the public, I wince and look around again. He knows talk of mermaids would get him ridiculed. Not that what he said is any less strange.

"If my father finds out you are here, we're both going to be in trouble," I say.

"I'm just a friend."

"A *guy* friend."

He scoffs. "I'm perfectly harmless."

"My father doesn't think any cute boy near his girls is harmless."

"I'm cute, am I?"

I open my mouth for a snarky comment, but I don't get the chance to utter a word. The front door opens with a screaming Abigail on the other side. I grab Stephen to ensure we're both well-hidden and peek out around the tree. Abigail mutters some strong curses and walks toward the side of the house. Before she disappears around the corner, I see her pull a cigarette out of her pocket. Another habit Dad would disapprove of, but I couldn't care less. Particularly now.

With the coast clear, I grab Stephen's hand and drag him away from the house at a jog. I turn down a side street and let go. He follows without being dragged. "Where are we going, Naomi?"

"Anywhere that my sisters or father won't see us," I answer.

"Did you eat yet?"

"Yes. We always have full family dinners."

"Dang. I rushed out here so fast I didn't get to eat. How about ice cream?"

I shutter at the memories of the accident when he mentions ice cream. I have a good excuse though. "I'm broke."

"My treat."

Stopping in the middle of the sidewalk, I turn to him. "You need to go home."

"We need to talk."

"Could have been done on the phone."

"Not with the state you were in last time. Fine, no ice cream. Any bakeries? I'll search myself if I need to."

I grumble but nod, taking him to the one I know that is least likely to get me into trouble. My eyes widen as he gets a slice of pie, a piece of pumpkin roll, and two chocolate chip cookies. I gaze over the selection at his prompt and choose a white chocolate macadamia cookie. One cookie makes me feel less guilty about his generosity and less annoyed at my father's stubbornness over my allowance. When he makes me choose a drink, I get a small sweet tea while he chooses the most heavily caffeinated soda available.

We slip into a table, and I get right back to trying to convince him. "You being here will only cause me trouble, Stephen. I'm fine."

He shakes his head and takes a bite of pie with a moan. "That's so good. Great choice. And not with how you sounded on the phone earlier. I took the first flight out here, hoping you would hold off the urge until I arrived."

My mouth twists in displeasure at my own weakness. "It was a bad moment. I don't feel any pull right now."

Stephen raises an eyebrow, as if to tell me he doesn't believe any of that. I break a piece of my cookie off and stick it in my mouth to give me an excuse to look away from his dark blue eyes. I was, in fact, lying. Distractions help, but the longer I'm away from the water, the worse it gets. At this point, there's always an aching desire. Even without knowing the town like the back of my hand, I could close my eyes and turn to face the direction of the beach without thought.

I bury my face in my hands and mumble through them. "I'm not sure we can win this."

"I'm not failing another person, Naomi. We will find a way. I still have feelers out for people who might have answers we can use."

"The forums?"

"Yeah. After you alienated the entire group, I decided to take on the quest to get answers from them. You'll be happy to know that they shut down commenting on yours and archived it at my request. No more death threats."

I laugh. "I haven't even paid attention lately. I have more things to worry about than children insulted that I don't believe in what they do."

"Do you still not believe?"

Sighing, I take a sip of my tea. Stephen lets the silence stretch. We haven't been talking all that long, but I feel he's picked up well on the cues that signal the need for a moment to compose my thoughts.

Not that I need to compose much. "It's hard not to at this point."

Pie done, Stephen starts on the pumpkin roll. "I figured, but I didn't want to assume. The idiots on the forums are just that—idiots. Don't worry about them. After how society treats the subject, we can't expect everyone to believe easily. It took me a bit to myself. Those coming for answers need understanding, not threatened or insulted."

"You're so level-headed. I was giving up hope of an answer before I found your reply. How did you find me?"

"Easy," he says with a shrug. "I searched the net for the attacks you told me about, the kid who lost his leg and the guy that lost his life. That gave me a place to start. Once I got here, I stopped in at the visitor center, picked up a pamphlet, and saw a Naomi as daughter of the mayor. A little more research told me where the mayor lives, and a little patience paid off. I'm just glad you were the Naomi I was looking for. I would have hated to run into your foul-mouthed sister instead."

"You call that easy? Professional stalker?"

"If they paid me for it, I could probably make a killing. But no, simply a concerned citizen. Do you have more sisters like Ms. Angry back there?"

"I have six sisters. All have different personalities, but four of them seem to like to make my life miserable."

"Six?!"

I hide my smirk under the rim of my cup. It's not like this is the first time I've seen this kind of reaction to the news. Seven is a lot of kids in our present day. Make them all girls, and we get a double shock.

After a few gulps, I put the cup down and look him in the eye with a seriousness that makes his wide eyes narrow. "You need to go. My father is protective of his daughters and has the power to screw up your life. Go home."

"Well, controlling seven girls must take a lot of time and effort, so I'll give him that. I'm not leaving though. If you want, I won't show up at your house again. I'll get a hotel and not come near you. If you think the urge gets to be too much, you call me, and I'll be ready to intercept you."

Sighing, I lean back. I can tell by the stubborn look on his face and the earnestness in his eyes that nothing I can say will convince him to leave. "What about work?"

"I told you I took some needed time off."

"I'm not a need."

"Maybe in your eyes."

We stare off for a few moments before I concede. "Fine. But no more surprise visits. Promise me."

"I promise to stay away unless it's needed. Unlike someone I know, I keep my promises."

I flinch and look away. "Sorry about that. My defiant stubbornness got the better of me."

"I've already forgiven you. I just couldn't let it go without a little teasing."

We toss our trash out, leave the store, and say our goodbyes before walking away in different directions. I never asked what hotel he's going to stay at, but I do know it'll be the furthest from the ocean. I'm sure I can figure it out. Not that I want to.

Since I know the way home, I let my feet take me while I go over the shock of him showing up like he did. Even with his determination to stop the mermaids from claiming another, I never expected him to come here. The fact that he went through so much trouble for me blows my mind. With him being easy on the eyes, I can't help but wish he could stay. I shake that thought away. I don't want Dad to find out and risk hurting Stephen in some way. It's better to keep our distance. This outing was risky enough.

Staring at my feet, I keep walking without thought, knowing I'll be home soon. My mind goes over everything that Stephen promises and all my doubts and worries that it is all hopeless. When I hear waves crashing, I jerk my gaze up. A few feet in front of me changes into the rough wood of the boardwalk. Beyond that is the one place I swore I wouldn't go.

How did I get here? I was walking home. Sure, I wasn't paying attention to where I was going, but I know this town well enough not to need to. My feet must have turned me around against my wishes. What the hell?

My only answer comes from the waves crashing in the darkness. Only the artificial lights give me the ability to see, but the view of the white tops of the waves still stand out in my vision. The smell of brine creates a longing so strong that I find myself taking a small step forward.

Fear leaps in my chest, and my hands tremble. I can't be here. This is dangerous. I turn and run the other way, making sure to pay attention to my direction this time. The ache in my heart brings tears to my eyes as I run in the opposite direction it wishes me to. This time, I make sure to pay attention to where my feet take me until I reach my front door, gasping for breath.

Chapter Twenty-Five
Fear for Another

I wake with a stretch, yawning while my spine realigns and my muscles loosen. A groan escapes my lips. The sun has yet to rise, so I lie in bed a little longer, soaking up the warm sheets and soft comforter instead of the cold, hard floor. After a bit, I decide I might as well shower.

I slip my phone into my pocket and leave in search of food. Plugging my ears to the shouts is difficult, but I manage to skirt around the pairs arguing in the early morning hallway. I weave around them and walk down the stairs. Someone says my name. I let it go in one ear and out the other. I'm in no mood for whatever torture they think to throw at me.

Emma is already painting in the living room. She gives me a smile and wave, which I return before turning into the dining room. Lucy has yet to claim the table for her books and notes. The kitchen radiates with silence for the moment. I have no doubt it won't last for long.

My eyes skim over the usual donuts and muffins. Inhaling deeply, I scowl at the muffins. I miss them so much. That thought alone makes my stomach do a flip. I'm not sure when I went from occasionally eating my old favorites to deciding they're not worth the risk of discomfort or taste of garbage, but I'm fully set in my new appetite. At least, I can still eat non-carnivore food if it's mixed with meat.

Which makes the finding of the last burrito all the sweeter. Of course, no sausage, but I'm sure eggs and cheese will still go down easy enough. Humming, I place the meal onto the tray and slide it into the preheated toaster oven. Next, I stick my head into the refrigerator long enough to locate the orange juice. My flavor issues haven't spread to liquid nourishment yet. Knock on wood.

The sound of footsteps reaches my ears as I'm returning the fruit juice to the fridge. I grimace and pretend to be busy. Maybe whoever it is will leave me alone if I'm in the middle of something.

"Naomi."

I grit my teeth at the voice that I feel is worse than all others. "Father."

Holding back an annoyed sigh, I pull my head out and look at the man in question. It's Saturday, but he is still dressed for success. There must be some sort of event going on, as usual. I can't remember the last time I've seen him in jeans or shorts.

"Hiding from me in the refrigerator?"

I hold back my wince before a single muscle can consider twitching with the urge. "I thought you were someone else."

The toaster oven saves me with a ding. I walk over and put my breakfast on a plate. Dad remains silent, but I can feel his eyes on me the entire time. In a hurry to get out of this shared space, I grab my plate in one hand and reach for my juice.

"What's this I hear about you having a date at the bakery last night?"

Damn it.

My hand stops halfway curled around my glass. "What date? I wasn't on any date."

"Councilman Derek saw you eating sweets with a young man that he described as attractive."

Of course he did. This is why I didn't want to go out in public with Stephen last night. Why couldn't he have just gone home?

"I'm waiting for an explanation, Naomi. This outing with a boy was not pre-approved."

I scowl at my hands. Why can't I be allowed to have a typical new adulthood? Most women's parents lay the hell off when she becomes an adult. Mine just buckles down harder.

"It wasn't a date," I say when my temper cools enough. "Stephen talked to me online once or twice due to similar fictional obsessions. He just happened to be in town, and I wanted to say hi—as a friend."

"What are your plans with him?" The stillness he exhibits goes beyond anger. He's steaming and ready to step in.

I shrug as nonchalantly as possible. "He's staying in town for a day or two to do some beach research and leaving. I won't be seeing him again."

It's not a lie if I don't know for sure, right? The fact that my father stiffens makes me frantically go over what I said. Beach. I mentioned beach. That was one of the dumbest things I've done in a short while, which is saying something.

"You went to the beach?" Father says, eyes turning dark and voice no longer cool.

I search for a reason that will calm him. "Not even close to it. We went no further than the bakery. I told him about our festivals and different events at the beach. I didn't go near it."

Okay, some of that is a flat out lie, but he doesn't need to know. Guilt for lying is absent when I'm doing it to save Stephen a hell of a lot of trouble. Tourist, that's what I'm making him out to be. That's fine with me. Better than my supposed boyfriend.

Dad looks suspicious, but I offer him my most innocent smile, surprised when he lets out all the tension in his body with a sigh of relief I doubt I'm supposed to notice. "If I hear anything else about this Stephen, there will be hell to pay, Naomi. Boys are dangerous."

"Of course. I have no interest in taking anything further. I was simply being a good friend."

He nods and turns to leave before pausing. "Take one of your sisters next time you meet a friend. It is unseemly to be seen with a boy on your own. You know how gossip flows."

"Of course."

Inside, I'm not as kind. *And you're the one listening to gossip and giving it power. Let me live my damn life, and things like this won't become an issue at all.*

As soon as he's out of the kitchen, I let out a pent up breath. It's hard paying nice when all I want to do is the opposite. If it was only for me, I wouldn't pretend at all. This isn't for me. It's keeping Stephen safe until he's out of the town and far enough away from my father that he's unable to touch him. I slip my burrito onto a plate, debate for a few seconds, then take it outside.

The air is cool this early in the morning, the sky slowly brightening into dawn. Over the birds exclaiming their love for the coming day, I hear a car engine. Dad is getting ready to leave for whatever. It's probably not even anything he has to attend. Anything to get out of the house full of bickering daughters.

Shrugging, I tell myself it doesn't matter. As long as he's not home, he's out of my hair. Just like I like him; leaving me alone.

Even without the meat, my breakfast goes down easily. Once done, I spend time enjoying the encroaching morning light while sipping my orange juice. A chipmunk skitters across the grass and into a hole under the gazebo. It's a pleasant early summer morning, and I plan to enjoy it as long as possible.

Clara destroys my peace by coming through the back door. Her lip curls in an unpleasant look that doesn't affect her beauty. She proceeds to one of the flowering bushes and starts taking selfies. Rolling my eyes, I stand and go back into the house, my peaceful morning shattered.

In my room, I send Stephen a text. *Someone saw us and told my dad. Please, go home before he does something to cause trouble.*

A few minutes later, my phone rings with a video call. I answer it, no longer worried about who he is. Stephen pops up on my screen, his eyes still heavy with sleep and his hair even more chaotic. This man sports some massive bedhead.

"I hope this is okay," he says. "I figured since we met in person, you know I'm not some kind of perv looking for kicks."

"I don't really know that yet, but I'm giving you the benefit of the doubt. Although, you're a dedicated perv if you are one."

Stephen smirks, and the background spins as he sits on the bed in his hotel room. He rubs his eyes. "How do you look as you do?"

My brow furrows. "What do you mean? Does something look wrong?"

He laughs. "Just the opposite. You look all put together, like you've been up for hours."

"I have been. Don't want to waste the day."

Dark blue eyes narrow on my screen. "So, you're one of them."

My heart skips a beat. Is something wrong? "One of who?"

"The dreaded morning person. The ignorant early riser who doesn't understand the wonders of sleeping in."

The mock severity in his tone makes me laugh, chasing away all anxiety. "You're awake too."

"Your text woke me. The only reason it took so long to call you is because I had to use the restroom."

"Oh, I'm sorry. I figured you'd put your phone on silent during sleep like a normal person."

"Normal person?" he asks with a grin. "This is coming from the woman who gets up at dawn."

"Before dawn actually."

"Not helping your case," Stephen says, making me giggle. "And as for your statement, I didn't silence my phone in case you had an emergency."

Realization hits me, and guilt takes over. He risks a disturbed sleep in case I need him to intercept a walk to the beach. Either he's taking this too seriously, or I'm not taking it seriously enough.

I press the persistent urge that he worries over down. "I'm fine. You need sleep."

"Not risking it."

Sighing, I plop down on my bed. A voice breaks through the walls surrounding me. Abigail, screaming as usual. Jumping back up, I hurry to the bathroom.

Stephen's eyes narrow. "I much prefer the view of the room. It's as neat as you are early at waking up."

"Are you going to be stuck on that?"

"Probably. If you need to use the bathroom, you could have told me and left me outside."

My cheeks heat. "It's not that. I heard one of my sisters. They won't hear your voice in here, so they won't tell Dad."

His lips press together in displeasure. "He keeps you on a tight leash."

I nod. "All of us. Controlling doesn't even begin to describe his tendencies to direct our lives."

"Why don't you leave?"

"I can't. He won't let me get a job, and he stopped my allowance after my last trip to the beach. He doesn't like me going there."

"I hate that I have something in common with someone like him, but at least my reason for you not going to the beach is for safety reasons."

"He claims the same thing."

Stephen winces. "Damn it."

I laugh. "If it's any consolation, I'm sure the reason for you worrying about my safety is probably better than his."

"I hope so."

With a smile, I open my mouth to tell him how he's nothing like my father, but nothing comes out. Stephen's eyes turn from amused to concerned. "Is everything alright?"

I want to tell him it is, but I can't. Only one thing causes lack of speech, so panic begins to rise within me with the extreme thirst. This has never happened during the day before. The earliest has been at supper time. Is it getting worse? Breathing stops.

"Naomi?!"

Tears stream from my eyes. I turn the phone away from my face because I know my teeth are no longer normal. I don't want him to see that part of me. Knees growing unsteady, I feel myself fall as the world starts to dim. I try to fight toward the tub, but the symptoms are coming too fast. Stephen continues to call my name from across the bathroom from where my phone skidded away during my fall. I can't answer. I can't move. I can't stay conscious.

Chapter Twenty-Six
Tails

The sound of dripping water breaks through the nothingness. I groan and resist opening my eyes. All I want to do is fade into oblivion. I don't want to do this anymore. Why did it happen while it was still light out?

A hand touches my face, startling me to open my eyes against my will. Stephen kneels beside the tubful of water that I'm now submerged in. "What are you doing here? You can't be here."

"I will be wherever I'm needed."

"How did you even get in? Please tell me no one knows."

Panic surges at the thought he may have casually knocked on the door. I'll never hear the end of this. His future is doomed to my father's anger. He has no idea what kind of shit storm he's released.

"Calm, Naomi," he says in a hush. "No one knows I'm here."

"How?"

He sighs and sits back on his heels. "You're going to call me a stalker again."

"Just tell me."

"Fine. I was going to anyway." He watches me with his dark blue eyes for a moment before getting into it. "The minute I realized what was happening, I took off. You won't be happy to hear this, but I chose the hotel closest to you to stay in. I needed to make sure I could reach you in a hurry, which I'm glad for now. When I found you, your lips were blue from drowning in the open air.

"Now to the more stalkerish part. I slipped into your backyard when I was sure it was clear, then I scaled the walls and looked for the room that was identical to the one I saw in our video chat. You really should start locking your window."

I stare at him in disbelief. This man slipped onto the property like some sort of spy, climbed a wall, then broke into my room. He did all this to help me. How did I find someone that feels I'm worth this trouble? It's too much.

"Who are you?" I whisper.

He laughs softly. "I'm not some kind of superhero if that's what you're thinking."

"I was thinking more along the lines of spy."

"Nothing that fancy. I'm a tech guy at an electronics store near the apartment I share with a knucklehead."

My expression is still one of wonder. "I'm not worth all that trouble."

Stephen's beautiful eyes grow sad, and he sits on his butt like he's tired of crouching. By the wince that comes with moving his legs, he probably is. All this discomfort for me, to make sure I survived. I still can't understand why.

He takes a deep breath. "At first, it was because I was determined to keep you from being prey to the mermaids. I still am because I won't let them claim another if I can help it. Once we started talking, I realized that you're a good person, if a little stubborn. Everything you've told me since I arrived showed me you deserve better than a life in the ocean, killing to survive. You also deserve better than the life you have here."

The earnestness in his voice brings tears to my eyes. "You hardly know me."

"I'm a people person. I know how to read people."

To lighten the mood, I scoff. "So you're one of those."

"One of who?"

"A people person. Someone who doesn't know the wonders of being alone."

Stephen laughs, but he does a good job of keeping it at a level no one can hear outside this room. "After my early riser comment, I deserve that."

"You sure do."

For the first time, I look over my body through the cooling water. My brows furrow when I realize I'm wearing a towel around my waist. That's when I remember my last episode ripping my pants. Horror rises in my throat.

Stephen must understand my sudden distress. "It's okay. You had a tail. I wrapped a towel around you before I put you in the water. I swear that I saw nothing. I'm not some kind of creep, breaking into bedrooms and ogling helpless girls."

I wiggle my toes to assure myself that I have legs again. "I had a full tail?"

"Yeah," he says, flinching.

"What did it look like? I've never been able to see it." This may be a strange question, but I can't help but ask it. Fear doesn't negate curiosity.

Stephen looks up at me with surprise. "Uhm, as much as I hate mermaids, it was beautiful. Your scales were an aqua-green color with purple shadings and purple fins. I wasn't expecting to find it pretty."

I feel a blush creeping up onto my face. Strange thing to be blushing over. It's not a common compliment, and I should be more horrified that he saw me at my lowest. Still, I can't stop my pleased smile.

Looking down into the water again, the smile falls. I'm now glad I told him that water helps me feel better and settle back to myself. This would be so much easier if I wasn't sitting in the tub with only a towel covering my lower half.

"Can you get me a pair of pants?" I ask.

"Sure. Where are they?"

"Dresser, third drawer down."

While a man I barely know goes to look through my dresser and dig through my clothes, I try to go over everything. It's getting worse. I've never had a full tail. Each time, it goes a little further. What happens when I can't turn back and die of suffocation? That thought makes me feel sick. It also happened during the day. So far, it's always been at night or evening and when I'm alone. What if I start mermaiding out in public?

When Stephen returns with a pair of sweatpants, I pose that last question. He purses his lips in thought. "I don't think you need to worry about that."

"Why not?"

"Mermaids use magic to hide from humans. They only allow humans they're interested in to see them. I'm not sure what's going on, but I doubt the magic they assaulted you with will let you be seen."

"You saw."

"Only because I rushed to see you before you could change back. It might have something to do with my sister letting me see you too. Maybe there's something special about me now."

"Special?" I say. "Like traveling across half the country to save a girl you don't know?"

He smiles and opens his mouth. A knock at the door interrupts whatever he was about to say. We both freeze.

"Noami! Open up!"

"Shit," I whisper. "That's Clara. Turn around."

Despite his bravado about not caring about being seen, Stephen has lost a little color. I'm not sure if it's more my warnings or the fact that he's in a strange woman's room with no clear indication of how he got here.

I step out quickly and drop the towel, pulling my pants on without thought. "Okay. Hide."

Stephen flattens against the wall beside the door, on the side where he won't be noticed. That's as good as it's going to get. I just need to make sure Clara doesn't burst in like she usually does.

The knock turns into banging. "If you don't open right now, I'm telling Daddy that you are refusing again when he gets home!"

Rolling my eyes, I open my door. When she tries to push in, I make sure to keep the door mostly closed to block her, which earns me a scowl. I offer a sweet smile that causes her to cross her arms over her chest while she tries to see what I'm hiding. I open the door enough to let her see my empty room but use my body to continue barring entry.

"What?" I ask.

"It's almost suppertime, and you're not down there yet. You're on fruit salad duty. You know how much work that is. Better hurry. If we're late eating because of you, Daddy won't be happy."

"I'll be down in a couple of minutes."

A smug look comes over her face. "Why can't you now?"

"Because I'm not ready."

She giggles. "Very well."

From the look of triumph Clara throws me before walking away, I'm sure she has something up her sleeve to get me in trouble. I close the door and try to talk my nerves into behaving. It doesn't work.

"She seems like a peach," Stephen says from the bathroom doorway.

"Story of my life." I hear a car pulling into the driveway, signaling Dad's return. He was out all day while I was unconscious for most of it. "You need to go. There's no telling what Clara will attempt, but I could tell she was planning something. He may come up here."

"One more thing," he says before making a move. He holds up my scale that was still where I last left it. "I found this behind your toilet. Can I borrow it?"

A shiver runs over my spine. The cause of all my troubles dangles from a shell necklace in his fingers. "Keep it for all I care. I want nothing to do with that thing. It's ruined my already dismal life."

Stephen hurries to my window and looks down after a sad glance my way. The coast is clear, but he turns back to me, taking my face in his hands. "I'm here to help, Naomi. Even if I have to shimmy up and down a drainpipe multiple times a day, I'm here. I won't let them have you. You're worth more than you can ever know."

I grab his wrists and smile. "If anything, you've proven that without a doubt. Thank you."

He stares into my eyes for a long minute before slipping out, finding the aforementioned drainpipe, and shimmying down, slipping behind the bush beneath my window. Like a super spy, Stephen moves from one hiding place to the next until he's out of sight.

Before closing the window, I take a deep breath of fresh air. Once closed, I move into the bathroom, pull the drain plug, and wring out the towel. As I'm hanging it on the rack, my door bursts open without so much as a knock.

Whatever I expected from Clara, it's coming to fruition now. I walk out of my bathroom to find Dad searching under my bed and behind my door.

"Can I help you?" I ask, ignoring Clara grinning from the doorway.

"Clara said you were hiding something. I'm here to see what that was."

I sigh. "I'm not hiding anything. You've destroyed anything I can hide."

"She said you wouldn't let her into your room."

Dad pushes past me. He checks the tub, behind that door, and the shower. When he opens the cupboard above my toilet, I hold my breath. A simple look seems to be all he needs because he closes it without rifling through the towels.

"It's my room," I argue. "She doesn't need to be in it. Besides, I'm tired of her stealing my stuff."

Clara rolls her eyes at me, but I ignore her. Father lets out a huff. "You were hiding your beach trips, your health issues, and seeing a boy. Stephen Moore. Don't think I don't have the resources to find out his identity. Why should I believe you now?"

Clara perks up at the mention of a boy, storing the information away for later use. That I'm sure of. I continue to ignore her and say, "The first one was the only thing I was hiding, and you didn't give me a choice. I figured you wouldn't care about the health part. The boy was simply information gathering. I haven't seen him since, so no reason to threaten his existence."

I'm getting too good at lying. I'd feel guilty if it wasn't for the man staring at me suspiciously. "Make sure you keep it that way," he says before leaving.

Clara looks disappointed when I shut the door on her face. I lean against it, glad I got Stephen out of here when I did. That was too close. I need to make sure not to have any more episodes while on the phone with Stephen. I can't risk him being caught in my room. I'd rather drown out of water.

Chapter Twenty-Seven
Uncomfortable Truths

In the middle of my latest chapter, my phone buzzes. I've been able to focus a little better today, but it takes me twice as long to finish a chapter. I've also switched from horror to fantasy with everything happening lately. Good thing I will read most genres. I still miss my horror.

I lift the phone and unlock it to see a text from Stephan. *We need to talk in person.*

Digging my teeth into my bottom lip, I let my fingertips hover over the letters. We shouldn't meet. I know this. He knows this. Something inside craves his presence, almost as strong as the craving to feel the tide between my toes.

Sighing, I type, *You know that isn't a good idea. I can hide out in the bathroom for another video chat.*

I could, but I want to talk to you face-to-face. This is an important and possibly uncomfortable conversation.

That helps my anxiety and makes me want to meet him in person. Sure...

It's not safe, I reply after a short pause.

What if we went somewhere out of town? I can have a cab meet you a few blocks from home.

Stephen has an answer for everything. Now, only my objection to the uncomfortable conversation holds me back. Stephen makes me feel safe and liked. I don't want to feel stressed around him. I mean, the mermaid stuff provokes plenty of anxiety. Even that can't make me feel less safe in his presence.

Fine, I type and send him the name of a diner too far for Dad's lackeys to bother.

He sends me the address to be for the taxi in thirty minutes. I glance at my phone. It'll only take me twenty to get there, but I should maybe leave earlier to give me time for any distractions. Slipping from my room, I find the hall empty. At the steps, I hear Clara telling Brooke to get over something. I hang back until both of their voices sound more distant.

Creeping down isn't suspicious at all, but I can't help going into stealth mode when someone else's life is on the line. I can see Clara and Brooke still arguing through the window on the front door, so I turn toward the dining room to use the back. Lucy stops studying and smiles at me. I haven't talked to her much lately and can't try to avoid it now without hurting her feelings.

"Where you off to?" my only quiet sister asks.

"Heading out to the backyard. I might take a walk."

"Not to the beach?"

I can understand her reaction between Dad's furious retaliations and her knowledge of the guy trying to hurt me last time. "Nope. Learned my lesson."

"Good. I don't like seeing you in trouble, and I worry about your safety. Do you need someone to come along?"

I guess I deserve this concern. It seems like most of the time I leave the house anymore, something bad happens. Lucy is smart enough to pick up on that.

Shaking my head, I grin at her. "I can handle it. Not that I wouldn't appreciate you coming. I just need some time in the fresh air with a little exertion to work through my thoughts."

"If you're sure..."

"I am."

She nods and turns back to her notes. That took half of my extra time, leaving me happy I allowed for it. I slip out the door and use the gate at the back of the fence. It takes an entire block for me to walk normal—not on a secret mission—again. No one saw me leave, except Lucy, and no one is following me. I take the next right and walk further away from the ocean that pulls at my heart more than a lost lover.

My phone tells me I made it with two minutes to spare, so I sit on the curb and browse my emails. The taxi pulls up five minutes late. I get in without question and close the door.

A few minutes later, Stephen sends me another text. *Make it?*

In the taxi and on my way.

He sends me a thumbs up emoji, and I go back to flipping through apps on my cell. The ride takes about twenty minutes, long enough to get mostly out of my father's influence. When I reach the diner, I find Stephen all the way in the back booth. He even left the side facing the wall for me, so no one can see my face unless they're right by our table. Now I'm sure he's some kind of secret agent.

I slide in, and Stephen smiles at me. He says, "I ordered you a sweet tea. I hope that's alright."

"My favorite."

"Thought so when you ordered it at the bakery."

I lift my menu and browse the options. At a lonely diner this distance from the beach, the seafood selection is slim. I frown and remind myself that moving away from the beach does this. A price for the added safety. This far, my heart is screaming at me to turn around and go back. Logic that it's dangerous that way is the only thing that keeps me from listening.

When the waitress brings my tea, I put the menu down and take a sip. She asks for our orders. Stephen takes a bacon cheeseburger and fries. I order the breaded shrimp and substitute the fries with cheese sticks. Any animal product seems to be better than anything else on the menu.

Stephen doesn't even raise an eyebrow at my choice. "How was your night?"

"Incident free."

"Good."

"What did you want to talk about?"

He's quiet for a bit. "I contacted the man that runs the website we met on. He seems like the closest thing to an expert we will find."

I snort to hold back my ironic laughter. Stephen doesn't react to it, knowing where my mind is heading. He's such an understanding person.

My first thought of that site and its admin was nutjob and conspiracy theorist. I'm not sure about the conspiracy right now because it still seems like a stretch that the government is hiding mermaid knowledge. I no longer think he's crazy for believing in mermaids and creating a space for other delusionals. I've seen too much to not believe any longer.

"What did the high and mighty mermaid expert have to say?" I ask.

"That someone has beaten the mermaid transformation before."

My drink is halfway to my mouth when I pause, the straw between my fingers and lips puckered for the reception of said straw. Can it be true? Is all hope not lost? Can I beat mermaidism or whatever it would be called? This is the best news I've heard since this all started.

"Keep your lips in that position, people will think you're a fish," Stephen says into my silence.

I scoff and take the sip of tea I was going for in the first place. "At this angle, no one can see my face but you. Also, I'm part fish at this moment."

His amusement sobers. "But you don't have to stay that way."

I open my mouth to respond but close it when Stephen shoots me a look. The waitress shows up two seconds later. She slips a very thick burger with fries in front of Stephen and my shrimp in front of me.

When I take a bite of a cheese stick, I can taste a small hint of rot in it, making me grimace. I start picking the breading off it. "Do you really think it's possible to stop this?"

"Jack seems to think so." When he takes in my quizzical eyebrow raise, he adds, "The owner of the website."

I take a bite of cooling, naked cheese, glad to find the nasty taste gone. "So what's the secret?"

Stephen watches me undress the next stick and shakes his head. "Stay away from the sea. That's what he says. We need to not let any part of you touch the water. It's the catalyst."

I laugh and take a bite of my newly freed stick of dairy. "We are already doing that."

"We keep doing it."

With a shake of my head, I pop the second half in my mouth and chase it with a sip of tea. "But staying away from the water isn't helping. You said that your sister only had problems when she was at the beach. I'm not the same. We've already established this."

Stephen licks his lips and looks down at the fry he's swirling in ketchup. Our conversation pauses as the waitress comes with drink refills. This gives him time to come up with a solution or argument.

As soon as she's gone, he says, "Maybe you just need to be further away."

"I can't really get any further."

Silence stretches, and Stephen drops the fry without eating it. His deep blue eyes find mine, and he takes a deep breath. It occurs to me that every part of this conversation so far hasn't infringed on the realm of uncomfortable. His preparation for what he's about to say tells me that part is coming. I brace myself.

"Come home with me," he says.

My mouth drops open. It takes a moment for me to realize I'm showing him half-chewed cheese and shut it. I finish chewing and swallow, moving to de-breading my shrimp next. Not even risking that flavor.

When I'm composed again, I take a deep breath. "That won't work, Stephen. My father holds all of my documents hostage."

"We'll get you new ones. You only have to stay until you can afford to move out and only if you don't want to stay with me."

I knew I could get new ones, but that was the easier excuse. Even the shrimp doesn't taste better right now, not with my nerves hiking up because of the bomb he just dropped on me. "I want to leave this all behind; you know I do."

"You don't trust me? I swear I'll be the perfect gentleman. I'll even make my roommate follow my example."

I scoff. "From what you've told me, there's no knocking him straight. The thing is, we both know what's happening to me isn't normal. Well, less normal than our lack of normality already. What if moving away only makes it worse?"

He sits back with a grimace. "We don't know it will get worse. For all we know, getting further away is all you need."

"And for all we know, it won't help at all. Every time it gets worse, Stephen. I've told you this, and you seem to understand. What if regular water isn't enough later? What if I eventually drown without saltwater? As much as I don't want to be a mermaid, I'd choose that over dying."

I know I kept my voice low enough, but I glance around to make sure no one heard my crazy talk. The diner is blissfully empty on this end. I think my point finally reaches Stephen because he grunts and pushes away his plate like his appetite has fled.

The waitress hurries over. "Is something wrong with your burger, sir?"

He shakes his head. "It's fine. I just had the appetite knocked out of me. I'll eat more in a bit."

"Okay. Well, let me know if something needs fixed."

"I will."

Silence stretches between us as she scurries away. It's a few minutes before he stuffs another fry in his mouth. "Okay. Here's what I'll do. Can you keep up avoiding the lure of the ocean for a little longer?"

"It's hard, but I can manage. I'm pretty stubborn."

"So I've noticed," he mutters, only a little disgruntled. "I'm going to message Jack again and give him more information. Are you alright with me giving details?"

I shrug. "At this point, what choice do I have?"

"Not much."

"That was a rhetorical question, by the way."

He takes a bite of his burger and chews. Whether his appetite is back or he's keeping up appearances, I'm not sure. I only have three butterfly shrimp left to take the breading off and eat. I'm ahead in this meal.

The waitress returns and looks at my plate with confusion clouding her eyes. "Something wrong with our breading?"

I shake my head and look for an excuse that might seem half normal. "I'm watching carbs."

She glances at my sweet tea with her eyebrow raised. I merely smile like a naïve idiot until she shakes her head and walks away with promises to bring me another glass of sugar. Not that she puts it that way. I can read between the lines.

"So, here is what we'll do," Stephen says, looking awfully amused. "I'll message this guy details and see what he has to say. I'll contact you as soon as he answers. He's not often available during the day."

I agree with his plan and finish my meal without looking at the waitress when she brings my refill. Stephen settles me into a cab that's taking me to a different point from my pickup, and I again wonder if he's some kind of spy. I can see why he wanted to speak in person. This wasn't a conversation that was best had over the phone. If only Jack has some answers for us.

Chapter Twenty-Eight
A Way Out

It turns out that it doesn't take long to hear from Stephen. I'm being punished with an extra night on cooking duty. This time, I'm on potatoes. I hate peeling potatoes. Their juice gets all over everything. It's aggravating, as is the feeling left on my hands when I'm done.

I cube the potatoes when the peels are off and place them in a pot of water for boiling. While waiting for the water to heat, I feel my phone buzz in my pocket. I squeeze past Lucy to wash white potato juice from my hands and pull my cell out to find a message from Stephen.

We need to talk in person again.

Sighing, I answer, *I can't right now. I'm on cooking duty.*

Can you get away after?

I lick my lips and poke a potato, knowing it's not done yet. *Maybe I can slip away when dinner is cooked, but I'll pay for it.*

As much as I don't want you getting in trouble, this is really important. Jack got back to me already. We need to talk.

His urgency isn't lost on me, so I agree to take the punishment for missing supper. This seems urgent enough to deal with it. It takes forever for the potatoes to soften enough to mash. While I add butter and sour cream, I keep glancing at the clock. It's moving slower due to my hurry to get out of here.

Salt and garlic go in next, then I use the electric mixer to mash everything together. Others are already taking their food into the dining room as I finish. Lucy comes back in to see if I need help.

"Actually, can you carry this in? I want to throw my hair up before I come in. Don't want Clara freaking out about me doing it around the food," I say, feeling slightly guilty for my lie.

"Sure."

Lucy takes the bowl without further question, intensifying my guilty conscience. I exit through the back door and slip on Emma's old flip-flops that she keeps for when inspiration asks for her to move her art endeavors outside. As soon as I'm away from my house, I text, *Where to?*

Same pickup. I found a seafood restaurant a little further out.

My distress over the breading must have not gone unnoticed. How could it have? Even the waitress remarked on it earlier today. Two meals out in one day. That doesn't happen often.

The taxi is already waiting for me. I slip in and ride it to the destination. It's a chain restaurant, but seafood is seafood. This time, I was in the car for thirty minutes. I step out to Stephen waiting by the door.

"We need more phone calls. What will people think?" I tease, trying to keep my nerves down.

"Maybe I'm enjoying your company."

I let out a nervous giggle, and we walk in. I go for a lemonade this time and something without breading. "What is so important?"

My stomach growls at this point. Stephen laughs. "Let's eat first. I need to interrogate you, so I need you focused. Let's settle your stomach."

"Yeah, my stomach is so gonna settle after that statement."

He reaches over to take my fingers in his. "This is good, Naomi. We may have figured out how to remove the abnormality from your lack of normalcy. But we need to brainstorm the exact cause, so we can confront it."

My plate arrives in front of me, but I can only stare at it at first. I chose the make your own plate with shrimp scampi and baked cod. There are also some fries I don't plan to eat. I scrape those onto Stephen's plate, earning a knowing smirk. He's paying for it. I'm not wasting it.

Things taste so much better without the distraction of breading, but I still stare for a few minutes without eating. Stephen notices and puts his fish sandwich down without taking a bite. "What's wrong?"

"Oh, I don't know. Maybe all this my fate hanging in my balance, but I can't know what it is without eating first."

"You need to eat. I promise fifteen or twenty minutes isn't going to hurt."

Since he has all the information, he would know better than I do, so I nibble at a piece of shrimp. As soon as the food hits my tongue, I find my appetite comes back full. The beast in me seems to be hungry, and we have unfettered shrimp.

I'm done before Stephen and sip my lemonade while he finishes up the extra helping of fries. I curse the restaurant's lack of flexibility. Why couldn't I have chosen a third seafood entrée instead of one of their disgusting side options? Nothing was meat of any kind.

Stephen leans back as he chews his last fry. "I'm stuffed."

"You shouldn't have pigged out on fries," I tease as well as I can with my anxiety climbing higher. I've never been good at waiting for important things, and this is one of the most important talks of my life. He needs to quit stalling.

My thoughts must show on my face because the laughter dies in his eyes, and he holds his hands up. "Alright. Alright. Let's get into this."

"Finally," I mutter, stopping as the waiter comes by to ask if we'd like dessert. Stephen is too full, and I'm sure asking for more shrimp for dessert would go over well. He asks for drink refills though, so we need to wait for them to arrive. My heart feels like it wants to explode with the need for answers.

"Okay," Stephen says after our waiter comes and goes. "So, Jack says what you are experiencing is, in fact, not normal."

I can't hold back my laugh. "No kidding. I hope there is better information than that."

"It's not unheard of though." My laughter dies down, and I wait for him to continue. "The fact that you are being triggered without the use of saltwater means there is another catalyst."

My brows furrow. "What catalyst?"

"That's it. He doesn't know. Some additional sort of magic that is pushing your transformation without the sea to do it for you."

I sigh. "This isn't helpful. What kind of magic?"

"He listed a few things. Maybe the mermaid is stronger. If that's the case, you're screwed because we can't stop it. Some get really nasty when their chosen human tries to run."

"Greeeaaat. Please tell me there are other options. You sounded too optimistic to ask me to dinner, only to condemn me to ocean life."

Someone sits at the table next to our booth, and I flinch. We will need to be extra careful to be unheard. Stephen glares at the happy couple and slips into my side of the booth. At least there is no one on either side of the booth itself.

"There is. He says the magic can come from an outside source. It can be a curse or simply an enhancement of some kind. Go over everything in detail again, starting with before you found the scale."

I do as he asks, starting with me slipping out of the house and sneaking to the beach. The treatment from my sisters darkens his blue eyes until they're almost black. My interaction with my father makes fire light in them.

When I get to the part of singing on the beach, he stops me. "You sing on the beach?"

I shrug, feeling my cheeks warm. "Just a little song my mom taught me to give thanks to the ocean. I'm not really any good. Multiple sisters have told me so."

"I doubt any of them know what they're talking about. It was most likely said out of jealousy."

Staring at my hands, I'm quiet for a moment. "The guy that tried to steal me away at the beach told me I had a beautiful voice, but I figured he was just trying to get me to do as he said."

"I'm sure your voice is stunning. I'd love to hear it sometime."

With a shake of my head, I laugh. "No. I don't sing in front of people."

"After everything we've been through, you don't feel comfortable enough yet."

"I never will because I don't feel my song or voice is all that great."

Stephen readies an argument but stops at a squeal behind me. We both turn enough to see the woman covering her mouth with both hands, her eyes wide. The man kneels beside her with a ring box.

I don't want to be a killjoy or judgmental, but he should have picked a nicer restaurant. Maybe this is her favorite. A group of waiters comes out to set ice cream with sparklers in it on their table. They do a little song, making conversation completely impossible. I growl, but it's lost in the noise.

After a few agonizing minutes, things calm. We wait a little longer for the waiters to return to work and for the couple to start sharing their ice cream before we feel safe enough to talk. Maybe public isn't the best place to have these discussions, but I'm not risking being found in my room. No invites to my private room.

I launch back into my story with Stephen nodding along. After I get through the first day, he stops me. "Hold up. What about this strange little shop?"

Blinking, I stop and consider his words. It does seem likely. "It's owned by a creepy woman, who seems to be stalking me. I can't get rid of her."

"She's the one that made the necklace?"

"Yeah, and she keeps giving me jewelry boxes to replace the ones I throw away because I don't want anything from her. I don't want to owe her."

"Maybe you already do."

"Wait, what?"

He purses his lips at me. "I'm not sure you'll believe me, but I think I deserve a little faith at this point." At my nod, he continues. "Sea witch."

I choke on the sip of lemonade I was in the middle of when he speaks those words. The couple beside us glances over with alarm, but I wave away the concern. Their attention is the last thing we need right now if we want to avoid straight jackets. My eyes water as I wait for them to go back to having eyes only for each other.

"Sea witch?" I ask.

"Told you it would be hard to believe. Sorry I almost killed you."

"I survived."

Stephen gives me a soft, uncertain smile, but I motion for him to continue. "Jack says he's found plenty of evidence that they exist. Some are good, but others... not so much. I'm not sure why this one is on land, but she might be one. Tell me in more detail about what happened."

I go through everything I can remember, leaving him looking skeptical. He asks, "Anything else? No chants or anything?"

Memory of that day blurs with everything going on with me lately. "She did murmur over the scale. I couldn't hear it."

"Did she take anything of yours?"

"My credit card?"

Stephen shakes his head. "It would have to be something she kept. No money? Okay, what about hair or anything directly from your body?"

I take a moment to think, and my eyes widen when it hits me. "When I took the tooth back, it pricked my finger, and I bled on the receipt."

"That's it. We're going back to town together."

He grabs my hand and pulls me from the booth. Having already paid, we don't need to wait. The couple sees our fingers wrapped together and our hurry, producing knowing smirks that make me blush. Well, they don't know what the real hurry is.

Stephen calls a cab while we wait outside. The sky is dark, not a single twinkling star. Clouds are never good for me. It seems like only bad things happen to me without the sun, particularly in town.

As the cab pulls up, Stephen says, "Now, for the hard part."

"This was the easy part?"

"Yes. Now we have to convince her to undo whatever she did. I have a feeling this won't be easy."

I slip into the backseat and slide over to let him climb in behind me. He's right, I just don't have the heart or courage to say so. Lenora isn't going to give up her grip on me without a fight.

Chapter Twenty-Nine
Unreasonable Witch

Rain hits the windows as we ride toward the destination that decides my future. That makes me feel a bit dramatic, but it's the truth. My life has taken a dramatic turn and won't stop, spiraling into a world of myth and magic. If I want this to end, we need to be successful here. I will make her undo whatever horrible spell she holds over me.

I tell the cab to stop without turning onto the side street that leads to her alley. Stepping out, I wait for Stephen to pay the driver. My eyes lead down the dark street in front of me while the light rain soaks through me.

My phone rings. Taking it out, I look to see my father is calling. I bite my lip and ignore the call, then slip the phone into my pocket. I'm sure he's fuming at my absence. At this point, I don't care. The end is so near. Tonight, hope is realized or lost. I'm determined for it to be the former, even if I must run away with Stephen to get away from the pull of the ocean.

The fact that this is undoable—not some angry magic from the mermaid because of rejection—I feel relief and hope for the first time in so long. Lenora will release me, and I'll do whatever I have to. I'll return to this street, mermaid episode free. I'll run off to keep the ocean away from me once the hold is broken.

My phone dings. I fish it out one more time to see a voicemail. Shaking my head, I lock the screen and put it away again. I'll deal with my punishment later. This is too important to let my father distract me from.

Stephen steps beside me and takes my hand. "Ready for this?"

I squeeze his fingers, marveling at how right this feels, standing next to him to face down a witch from the ocean. Maybe I will accept his offer. He lives in the perfect place, as far from the ocean as possible.

The ache in my heart makes me frown. This time, it isn't because of the urge to run to the waves and give myself to the creature who wants my future. The beach has always been a part of me. I've always felt a pull toward it, long before the pull turned into compulsion. My fondest memories take place walking along the sand with my mother. The plans I had to refill our collection can only take place on the wet beach in the morning.

It's either leave the beach, or give myself to the mermaids. Mom would understand.

"Naomi," Stephen says.

I jerk out of the dark parts of my mind, remembering he asked me if I'm ready. "Can anyone be ready to confront a sea witch that put a spell on them? Let's get this over with."

He squeezes my hand. "We will convince her. It doesn't matter what it takes."

Nodding, I take the first step. Stephen feels the tug of my hand with the movement and follows without another word. At the alley, I pause. It's dark and creepy, as if full of seething monsters. While not raining hard, the precipitation still gathers in small pools along the way. Who knows what might be hiding in the shadows?

Stephen squeezes my hand to bring me strength. Squaring my shoulders, I start down the dark alley. There are no monsters greater than the one we came here to confront. This is an evil woman willing to throw the life of a stranger away for whatever reason. I'm sure it's not great enough to absolve her of any kind of guilt. I've been through so much, and it's all her fault and the mermaid in question.

At the end of the alley, her shop lies dark. Either she's gone or went home. I don't know where this woman lives. If she isn't here, how will we accomplish my freedom? My chest thumps with the thought of coming this far for nothing.

Stephen steps forward and squeezes the handle to release the catch. The door swings open. No matter how crazy she is, she wouldn't leave her shop open for just anyone to come in. She's here. It's simply a matter of finding her.

We pause inside the door to let our eyes adjust to the greater darkness. The shelves stand like silent sentinels, strewn with wares for sale that are currently darker lumps in the shadows. I let go of Stephen's hand long enough to turn the full way around slowly. Where is she?

As if I said that out loud, a candle flares to life at the far end of the counter. Lenora grins at me from the circle of flickering light, letting sharp teeth show. I shudder at the sight and reach for Stephen's hand again. He takes it, whether to reassure him or me of the upcoming success, I'm not sure.

"Naomi," Lenora says. "What a nice surprise!"

Her dark eyes flash a strange shade of purple. I take a deep breath to steel my nerves enough to move forward. Stephen keeps to my side, as if he's a shield. I'm sure he feels like he is.

"What did you do to me?" I ask.

"Whatever do you mean, child?"

I clench my teeth. "You know exactly what I mean."

She smiles, revealing more teeth. They aren't like the mermaid tooth. Hers are more triangular, like a shark's but rounder. Her eyes turn purple for longer before reverting back to the darkness they've been every other time I've seen her.

"So, you've figured it out," she says, leaning back to gaze over us with a satisfied smile. "I was starting to think you would never even guess the truth. You're either stubborn or stupid, maybe a little of both. Unless you had help?"

Her cold gaze moves to Stephen, and I feel his shivers through the grip he holds on my hand. I take a deep breath, holding back the fear this woman provokes. I can't let her see it.

"What do you want to release Naomi?" Stephen says before I can.

She laughs. "Young man, I have no desire to release her. She is the only way I can get what I want. I've waited too long as it is."

"What do you want?" I ask.

Her purple gaze turns back to me, not changing back this time. "Revenge, my dear."

"I have no wish to be used for someone's vengeance. I'm my own woman."

She laughs. "Since when have you ever been your own woman? You're nothing but the property of Travis Morgan, mayor of this beachside town and complete idiot."

My back stiffens. She can say what she wants about my dad, but I won't take her insults to me. "I belong to no one."

"Is that so? Why don't you have a job or money? Why does Stephen's presence here scare you so? Why haven't you been at the beach as often since your beloved father destroyed your original beach treasures?"

Coldness takes my breath away. Blinking, I stare at her, no longer able to hold back the fear that turns my mind frantic. She knows so much more than she should. I've never told her any of that.

"How do you know my name?" Stephen asks.

Lenora smirks and echoes my thoughts. "I know so much more than you can ever guess. Your heart longs so much for the ocean that stole your sister, but you're too much of a coward to do anything about it."

Stephen's grip on my hand turns into a vise. It's uncomfortable, but I feel like this sensation is the only thing still grounding me. The panic surges inside me, and my body trembles.

"I'm not yours to use like a disposable tool," I say to take her attention from the man beside me.

She chuckles and reaches under the counter. "You signed a contract giving me complete control over your transformation, Naomi."

"I did no such thing."

Lenora places the paper on the counter, and it slides to me as if from an invisible hand. "You did."

I look at it, seeing strange letters I don't recognize. All that I find familiar is my signature at the bottom and the splotch of blood next to it. "I didn't sign this."

"Look closer."

It's hard in the mostly dark, but I notice imprints of numbers pressed into the small slip of paper. That's when I realize what happened. "That was a carbon copy of my signature. I signed the receipt, not this!"

"Magic cares not for the method that comes with the signature, not when it's reinforced with blood."

The paper disappears from my hand and returns to her. "This isn't fair. I didn't agree to anything."

"I have a paper that says otherwise. That's all that matters."

Stephen steps forward. "That's not all that matters. Naomi didn't agree to any of this, so you have to release her."

Her gaze twitches back to him, but it returns to my face again. "I need to do no such thing. They will pay for what they've done to me."

"Who?"

"The mermaid prince, for starters."

I jerk with surprise. "He's the mermaid who gave me his scale?"

Lenora rolls her eyes. "Merman. If you're going to be one of us for the short time I allow, you might as well get it right. Mermen are the males of our species. Mermaids are the females or the species as a whole."

"The short time you allow?"

"You'll find out soon enough, child. The other part of my vengeance is your father."

"My father?"

She cracks another smirk. "Yes. The prince banished me from the sea because I rebelled against the rule of his mother. Only the royal family has magic strong enough to do that to me. Your father took a golden opportunity and threw it away."

"What opportunity?"

"Power," she whispers over the short distance between us. "I would have given him the world if he would have accepted me and gave me his very extensive means and influence. He refused, so I cursed him."

I freeze, staring at her in shock. Dad does know this woman for reasons other than professional. "What was the curse?"

"Nothing too hard to accomplish. He's no longer able to father male children, and one day, one of his daughters will be stolen by the sea. You were perfect for the second part of it. The prince is enamored with your singing."

"My singing?"

She frowns. "I find myself growing tired of this conversation. It's hard conversing with someone with little wit behind their words. Quite boring. Now that you're here."

Lenora stands, and Stephen steps between us. "I refuse to let the waves take another woman I care about. A simple sea witch won't take that from me."

She scowls. "Simple sea witch? The insults from someone who doesn't deserve to share the same space with someone of such power. I'm so much more than you could even fathom, the woman who should have been queen of the sea. I'm more powerful than you can ever understand, mortal. Get out of my way, and I won't hurt you too much for the insult."

"Naomi, run," Stephen says before pulling some sort of weapon out of his pocket. I can't see what it is in this light.

"Have it your way, human," Lenora says with a pleased grin. "I didn't want to let you off easy anyway."

Her hair changes from black to steel gray, and her purple eyes glow. Stephen yells for me to run. When she waves a hand, he slams against a shelf, knocking it into the other and turning them into a short domino train. She practically glides over to him, sinking her sharp teeth into the place where his shoulders meet his neck. The smell of blood overwhelms me, and my feet finally unfreeze.

Flinging the door open, I rush out into the night. Tears for the man who sacrificed everything for me run down my face. I press hard to get out of the alley, splashing in growing puddles as I go. Something slams into my body, and the familiar darkness takes over.

Chapter Thirty
Plans and Executions

The sound of waves crashing and the smell of saltwater bring me back to the world of the living. I cough and sputter. Everything feels hazy. In what feels like the distance, I hear a beautiful voice singing a familiar song. It's stunning and mesmerizing. My vision slowly clears to reveal my doom.

Lenora stands in front of the water, singing a song that should never come from someone as evil as her. Her beautiful voice rises and falls, perfect in pitch. It's mournful and joyful at the same time. If the rest of my situation wasn't so apparent, I could find myself straining to hear it longer.

Watching, I can see the rain has stopped to let the moon shine through to give the tops of the rolling waves a glow. I'm under the pier, my feet bare and my hands tied behind my back. What I see making its way for me turns me frantic, so I pull and try to use the pier to saw through my bindings. About fifteen feet from my toes is the water.

And the tide is coming in.

From the feel of dampness of the wood holding me, I can already tell the tide comes in this far. I fight as hard as I can, but I can't break free.

"You're awake," Lenora says. "I was hoping the magic I threw at you wasn't too strong. We don't want you to miss this."

"Miss what?"

Lenora flips something in her fingers and looks back at the sea before turning back to me. The look of triumph is too much. I glance out over the water to see the familiar shimmer in the distance. My heart stops.

I no longer care what she doesn't want me to miss. "Let me go, please. You can't do this."

"Seeing how you're tied up, I don't think you have a say. I can do whatever I want. Humans are so pathetic. Living among them this long leaves me with a rage I can't quench. I soon get to unleash my vengeance against multiple opponents. Glorious."

"If you think this is going to hurt my father, it won't. He doesn't care what happens to me."

She smiles again. "You actually believe that, don't you? Do you realize your father knows of the curse? It's one of the reasons he has never retaliated against me for everything. He knows enough to fear me, as he properly should. Did you ever think that his nagging might have actually been because he was trying to keep you away from the one place you shouldn't go?

"All that control means nothing when one of his brats was determined to thwart it at all costs. He failed, but then again, you were born for the sea. I could feel it in you from the moment you were born. I simply had to wait for it. As for not caring, maybe he was trying to create distance in case I won. He'll learn it's not that easy."

I pull hard enough on the ropes that my shoulder wrenches. "All this because he wouldn't love you."

Annoyance flashes in her eyes. "Who said anything about love? I said power. I have no use for love. Humans and the weaker mermaids look for that, which the prince will come to regret. Falling for someone because of their voice..." She scoffs and rolls her eyes to tell me what she thinks of that concept. "I'm not so weak-willed. This town should be mine, at the very least. I'm made for greatness, and I will prove that.

"Love... So useless. Your father loved his wives, if you can believe that or not, particularly your mother. She was so pretty with her red hair and blue eyes, and you look so much like her it makes me sick, which is why she died faster than the others."

"You killed our mothers?"

Lenora laughs. "Don't be so naïve. Why are you so shocked? Of course I killed them. I couldn't let my rivals get away with turning your father's eyes away from what I had to offer. Your mother was so much smarter than you. Your father... not so much. You get your looks from your mother and your brains from your father, I think."

"You need to let me go. Someone might come along."

She shakes her head. "Do you really think I can't handle them? Here. If you think a human, or multiple humans, can stop someone like me, try to call for help." She tosses my phone at my feet. "If you can figure out how."

The tide is bringing the saltwater closer. Panic is too light of a word to describe what I'm feeling right now. I've gone from hopeful to hopeless. I need to get out of here. What happened to Stephen?

Tears fight for dominance, but I push them away. Now is not the time. Stephen came to save me, but he lost himself in turn. I can't let his sacrifice be in vain. I push away the memories of him telling Lenora that he cared about me. I can't focus on that right now.

Would killing the witch break the spell?

I almost laugh. How would that help me in the position I'm in? Even if I can break free, how can I kill her? I've seen how strong she is. I'm doomed. My gaze falls to my phone. Why would she even bring this?

Light blares from the boardwalk. I hope for rescue but know she's right. No one can stop her.

Lenora smiles with pure triumph, turning my blood cold. "It's about time." Looking at my confused expression, she chuckles darkly. "That man has so many hidden GPS applications on the phone that you'd never get them all."

Realization hits me as my father comes into view. She used my phone to lure him here. Of course, he'd come looking for me the moment he realized I was at the beach. He can't stand the thought I'd defy him again.

My neck hurts from being twisted far enough for me to look back and watch his approach. "Naomi, what have I—?"

His feet stop in the sand when he realizes I'm not relaxing and watching the waves. Lenora steps into view. "Travis."

Dad tenses at her appearance. "Lenora, what have you done to my daughter? You will pay for this."

"As if you can do anything about it. Besides, *you* did this to your daughter with your rejection of true power instead of the pathetic authority you hold now."

"Rejection is no reason for stealing a man's daughter."

When she starts laughing, he rushes at her. One wave of her hand throws him across the sand. He grunts when he lands. Lenora uses magic to drag him back and position him behind me, on the same pole. She even manages to tie our hands with the same rope without breaking a sweat. We are not winning this one.

"Dad," I say.

"I'm sorry. I should have warned you. But I was afraid knowing they're real would have made you more insistent to come. I really was trying to protect you."

I have no words in return because I can't argue with that. There's nowhere in my many childhood years that I'd ever believe mermaids to be some scary predator. He's right; I would have tried to find them.

"What are you doing, Lenora?" my dad says in his most mayor-like voice.

"You're going to watch your daughter die, Travis. I'm going to use her to lure the prince close enough to ambush him. Surprise will give me the upper hand I need. As soon as the water touches her toes, she'll start to change for good. There will be no turning back this time. The thing about this part of the pier? The water only reaches far enough to get her wet up to the waist. It won't touch her gills. She'll drown outside of the water, and you get to witness it all after I kill the prince for what he's done to me."

"You bitch," Dad roars. "I'll rip you apart."

I startle at his anger. This doesn't sound like anger over her taking something he sees as property. This is pure rage born from not wanting to lose me, let alone watch it happen.

Lenora ignores him and shows me what is in her hand. "Look familiar?"

Dad yells behind me, "What is it, Naomi?!"

The purple shell gleams in the light coming from Dad's car lights. When I notice the chip and crack in the corner, I gasp. "That's the shell I found at the beach last time I was here. I thought I lost it."

"You did," she replies. "I found it when everyone was going crazy over the death of the man who thought he was a predator. He learned he was wrong, didn't he? But I'm the greatest predator of all. Did you recognize my voice earlier?"

When my face shows my confusion, she sighs. "Pathetic. It was your voice, Naomi. It was the voice that captured the prince's attention. Since you were singing while holding this, I was able to trap your voice in it to use. He thinks you'll be the perfect princess. You're only bait. The weak don't deserve the mantle of royalty."

She walks back to the water's edge and starts singing again. That's not me. It can't be. There's no way my voice sounds that beautiful. When the glimmer shows in the water again, I realize it must be true.

I use the distraction to talk to my dad. "Why did you think to look for me?"

"That boy you were with, Stephen, called me. Apparently, he was able to use our library computer system to find my cell number. Smart kid. He told me you were in trouble but wouldn't answer when I asked for more information."

"Is he...?"

"Dead? I couldn't tell you. I called an ambulance and sent them to the library. That's all I can offer you."

"We weren't dating, Dad. He lost his sister to the mermaids and was trying to help me."

"Let's worry about this later."

I feel something cool near my toes. Looking down, I see the edge of the water receding, the sand newly wet only an inch from my skin. I squeak and wiggle my feet up until my knees are pressing against my chest.

"Naomi, speak to me. What is it?"

"The water is going to touch me soon," I say with a sob.

"We'll find some way out of this."

"I don't see one."

When I look at the waves, I see the shine is closer. Lenore is using what she says is my voice to lure the prince in. She's going to win this all around. If he thinks it's me, he may not be aware of her presence. I need to do something. At least one part of her plan needs to fail.

Then I realize there's only one thing I can do. "We have to keep her from killing him. Maybe she'll keep me alive longer to realize her plan. We need to warn him."

I open my mouth to yell at the approaching merman. Nothing comes out. In a panic, I look down to see the water touch my toes and backtrack. Pulling against the ropes makes my father grunt because I pull his arms back when I try to pull forward.

"Naomi?!" Lenora stops singing and looks back at my father's cry. Her face brightens with a smirk before she goes back to the first part of her plan.

The thirst hits me so hard I gasp. I can hear Dad screaming behind me but can't make out the words above the pounding in my head. I can only hope it's for the merman and not being wasted on me. I'm done for now because I can't avoid the sea. Stephen would understand. That thought brings more tears to mingle with the ones caused by my inability to breathe. She can't be allowed a complete win.

Tears stream down my face as the itch starts and my heart pounds painfully. Tearing fabric echoes when my legs start to fuse together. I can't see them through my blurry vision, but I can tell the transformation is complete now. I'd see a fin if I could look.

Lenora screams as my vision starts to grow fuzzy. I want to cry out in fear but can't with no air in my lungs. The bitch keeps screaming until I hear a thump in the sand. My hands fall, as if released from their bonds.

A blurry form appears in my vision. "He heard, Naomi. He was able to surprise Lenora and kill her by throwing her own magic back at her. We need to get you away. Please, talk to me," my father says, his voice breaking.

I have no way to answer, and all my limbs grow weak as my mind grows light. Then I hear a voice in my head. *No. She will die.*

When I hear Dad's voice, I realize the voice is in his head too. "I won't let you have her."

It's either me or death. If you love her so much, do you want her to die just to keep her? That's what will happen unless you bring her to me.

Father sobs and lifts me into his arms. I feel more wetness hitting me and gain a little reprieve from the pain. I still can't breathe, and the darkness grows.

I hear my dad's voice. "I loved your mother the most, which made me love you more than your sisters. I wish I was better at showing it. Losing you will break my heart, but I can't let you die. Not like this. Not because of my actions. I'm sorry for who I was to you.

"This is all my fault. I should have left when Lenora spoke of the curse, but I was selfish and didn't want to leave the town I had so much authority over. You were right about one thing. I put my mayorship over your safety. I really thought I could control this. Now, we're both paying for my greed and stupidity."

Salty water plunges around me, and my breath comes back. I gasp water into what I assume are my gills. My father is visible just above the surface. He hangs his head and walks away. His profession of love takes me by surprise. He needs to know I heard him. Mermaids can do that, right?

You can't yet. I will let him know.

When Father pauses to look back, I assume he now knows. A hand grips mine and pulls me into deeper water. The longer I'm in the ocean, the clearer my mind gets. I really want to say something to him. I can see his shape far away.

Stephen's sister showed herself to him.

The hand pauses in its pulling. *She probably had already fully accepted the change, which will happen once you accept my kiss. The strain you've dealt with will slowly ease and allow you to feel your magic, and my kiss will seal it. Lenora almost killed you, which weakens you. I'd kill her more painfully if I could.*

I turn and find a man floating in front of me. His hair is as dark as the ocean around us, with eyes a brilliant green. Reaching up, he touches my cheeks with fingers tipped with scale claws. His smile is full of sharp teeth like the one hidden in my towel cabinet. When I look down, I see we are both naked from the waist up, with scales trailing up to our chest. Like Stephen said, my tail is aqua-green and purple. The prince's is shades of blue and green. I'm fully a mermaid.

You're mine, he says into his head.

I refuse to belong to anyone anymore.

I'll make sure you want to be mine. Our society is matriarchal, and we cherish every female. Let me prove that to you. Maybe you'll let me hear your voice under the water.

He pulls me again, further into the depths. I take one last look back, but my father is gone. He sacrificed my presence for my life.

EPILOGUE

Stephen

Please, let me see you.

Unlike last time, my query is nowhere to be seen. Damp air blows into my face on the edge of the pier. My eyes strain for any sign of the woman I came here to save, the second one I failed. All that greets my searching eyes are waves rolling and crashing.

It's been a couple of weeks since she was taken. I spent most of that in the hospital. The rest of that time was used to gather whatever information about what happened that I could.

Travis Morgan was unreceptive to any form of contact until I was able to corner him at home. The fact that he didn't have me arrested for breaking and entering shows me how broken he is. News reporters salivate over his resignation. He's hidden away and is unwilling to talk to anyone. I barely got what happened out of him.

Naomi thought her father hated her, didn't care whether she lived or died. Nothing he's done ever opposed that thought. It's too late now. He waited too long to say it.

While there, I was accosted by one of Greta's sisters, who had paint all over her. She wanted answers I couldn't give. Nothing believable anyway. The others didn't mind her absence, but one shy woman had puffy red eyes. I wish I had something to tell them to make them understand.

When the next gust of wind picks up, I close my eyes to the salty spray. I'd be lying if I said I didn't miss this. Too many memories cloud the small bit of joy I feel, too much pain. I had hoped for so much more this time.

I wanted to save Naomi. I wanted to show her she's more than she believed. Now, she's gone, just like my sister. The difference is she's not showing herself to me.

Once more, I scan the horizon. A faint greenish purple shimmer greets my searching eyes. I whisper, "Naomi?"

It fades, leaving only the ocean in the sunset and the sound of a song in my mind. It caresses me with enough emotion to bring tears.

Reaching into my pocket, I pull the scale necklace from my pocket. It's my last remembrance of the woman I've come to care about. With a deep breath, I throw it through the air. It lands with the barest thunk, heard under the crashing of the waves.

The taxi beeps from the end of the pier. It seems they're here to take me to the airport. With a sigh, I turn my back on the water, rub the area on my shoulder that still pains me after Lenora's bite, and walk toward my chariot away from the sea.

I hope I never see another ocean in my life.

Follow the Author

For more information on Jessie Roberts and upcoming titles,please visit:

Facebook: https://www.facebook.com/Jessie-Roberts-101702305830874

Instagram: https://instagram.com/authorjessieroberts

TikTok: https://www.tiktok.com/@authorjessieroberts

Jessie Roberts can be contacted at jessierobertsbooks@gmail.com